I0823196

Romantasy Cocktails

Jassy Davis

Illustrations by Louisa Maggio

CONTENTS

WELCOME

If you've fallen in love with romantasy and long to bring some of that glittering dark magic – and smut – into your real life, this book can help. Transport yourself to a magical realm by mixing drinks inspired by your favourite tropes, characters and settings. *Romantasy Cocktails* has a libation to suit every taste – whether it's wicked or wonderful.

Those hankering for a wintery fae realm, look no further than a Woods in Winter (page 29). If you're yearning for a dark and brooding lover who goes completely feral at the thought of someone else laying a finger on you, make yourself a Shadow Daddy (page 45), a Jaw Flexer (page 91) or a Feeling Territorial (page 25). Long to be swept off your feet by a fine fae lord or lady? Shake up a Starlight Pool (page 21), a Kiss in a Rose Garden (page 87) or a Summer Ball Sangria (page 132). For the dragon obsessed, there are spiced cocktails that billow smoke like Dragon's Breath (page 50). Fans of werewolves and shifters will love a Pack House Punch (page 127) or a Serpent's Smile (page 76). While those who long to be bitten by a vampire should check out the recipe for a Sangarita (page 53) or Bite My Lip (page 84). And would-be witches can brew their own potions and impress their spicy book–loving friends with their newfound powers – check out Glamour Potion (page 34).

If you're new to making cocktails at home, the opening chapters explain techniques and equipment that will help get you started. Then all you need to do is pick your dream scenario, preferred ingredients and then mix a drink to match.

The Essentials

Choose Your Glasses

The right glass for the right romantasy cocktail makes all the difference. Stemmed cocktail glasses stop your hands from heating up the drink. Coupes ensure you breathe in the drink's aromas every time you take a sip. Old-fashioned glasses, also known as double-rock lowballs, are great for building drinks in the glass. The following glasses are best suited to the cocktails in this book. The sizing below is an average collected from a few different sources; the accuracy of the measurements will depend on where you live.

Highball & Collins Glasses

Highballs and collins glasses are tall, chimney-shaped glasses. The difference is that highballs are thinner and smaller. They're usually 240–350ml (8½–12fl oz) while collins glasses measure 350–450ml (12–16fl oz). If you want to invest in just one tall glass, pick a 350ml (12fl oz) glass, which will cover most options and can also stand in for a hurricane glass.

Nick & Nora, Coupes & Martini Glasses

Nick & Nora glasses are bell-shaped glasses that are named after characters in the 1930s movie *The Thin Man*. They hold 120–140ml (4–4¾fl oz), so they're great for small, strong cocktails that wouldn't fill a full-sized coupe.

Coupes – or champagne saucers – are stemmed glasses with wide bowls. They normally hold 180ml (6fl oz) – larger than a Nick & Nora – and are a great choice for shaken cocktails. The wide surface area lets the cocktail breathe and means you get the full force of the drink's scent every time you take a sip.

A V-shaped martini glass can be anything from 120ml (4fl oz) to a massive 250ml (8¾fl oz). With cocktails that are served up (without ice) in a stemmed glass, bigger is never better. The longer the cocktail sits in the glass, the warmer it becomes. Avoid oversized martini glasses and pick something on the smaller size. Better to have two delicious cold cocktails than one sad tepid drink.

Rocks & Old-fashioned Glasses

Lowball tumblers come in two basic sizes: single rock and double rock, which is better known as an old-fashioned glass. Single rock glasses are 250–300ml (8¾–10fl oz) and will comfortably fit a chunk of ice and your drink. Old-fashioned glasses are 300–350ml (10½–12fl oz) and they make great midsize glasses for liquor-forward drinks served over ice or cocktails served with crushed ice.

Flute Glasses

For sparkling wine cocktails, you'll probably want to use flute glasses. They normally hold around 180ml (6fl oz), and the shape of the glass is meant to keep the bubbles fizzing. Coupes, by contrast, expose the surface of the drink to more air, which opens up the flavour but dampens the fizz. For the best flow of bubbles, go for a flute.

Hurricane & Shot Glasses

These two glasses sit at opposite ends of the spectrum. Hurricane glasses are huge, usually around 600ml (21fl oz). They are named after hurricane lamps and are supposed to have been developed in New Orleans in the 1940s. It's the go-to glass for Tiki drinks and cocktails with a tropical flourish.

A standard shot glass, by contrast, holds 30–45ml (1–1½fl oz) while a double shot glass is 60ml (2fl oz). For the shot recipes in this book, the larger size is usually the better option.

How to Layer a Drink

Whether it's a shot or a long drink, the most important thing to remember when making layered cocktails is that 99 per cent of it is down to the density of the liquids you're using.

Drinks that are high in sugar and low in alcohol, like grenadine syrup, are normally heavy and will sink to the bottom of the glass. Sweet liqueurs come next. Fruit juices also float above syrups. Spirits are normally the lightest ingredients in a layered drink, although cream will also rise to the top.

The simplest way to layer liquids is to hold your barspoon upside down in the glass at a 45-degree angle, making sure it's touching the side of the glass and just touching the surface of the liquid. Slowly pour the drink over the back of the spoon. The bowl of the spoon should disperse the drink, so it forms a layer. Repeat as needed.

How to Smoke a Cocktail

There are two basic types of cocktail smoker to choose from: a smoking gun or a smoke lid. A smoke lid is cheap and easy to use, but a gun can be useful for doing several cocktails at once.

Smoke lids look like wooden spaceships. They have a chamber in the middle where you add a pinch of wood chips. Place the lid on top of your cocktail glass and then light the wood chips with a cook's blow torch. Cover the chamber and let the smoke fill the glass for 30 seconds to 1 minute – depending on how heavily smoked you want your drink. Then remove the smoker and serve.

Most smoke lids come with a mix of wood chips to choose from. You could use oak chips for Dragon's Breath (page 50) to give it a classic wood-fire flavour.

Once you've smoked your cocktail, make sure you put out the smouldering wood chips before throwing them away. You want your cocktail to smoke, not your whole house.

How to Make Citrus Wheels, Slices & Wedges

A wheel is a round slice of citrus fruit, a slice is half a wheel, and a wedge is a thick chunk of fruit. Use a small, sharp knife to cut wheels and slices from your fruit, around ½cm (⅕in) thick. With wheels, you can make an incision halfway into the round to make it easier to bend around the glass. For slices, just cut your wheel in half. To make a wedge, cut your fruit in half then cut each half into quarters lengthways. Larger fruits, like grapefruits or big oranges, can be cut into six or eight wedges.

Garnish with a Twist

One of the most common cocktail garnishes is a citrus twist – a strip of lemon, lime, orange or grapefruit peel. The easiest way to make a twist is to use a canele cutter/channel knife or a vegetable peeler. Simply pull the cutter along the skin of your citrus fruit to create a long, thin ribbon of peel. Add it to your drink just before serving.

How to Express a Twist

When you express a twist, you're extracting the citrus oils from the peel and misting it over the cocktail, which adds aroma to your drink.

Use your thumbs and forefingers to hold the twist over your cocktail, skin-side down, then gently twist it. An almost invisible mist of citrus oil will spray over the surface of the drink. Then rub the twist around the rim of your glass to coat it in the aromatic oil.

Drop the twist into your glass and serve.

Brew Your Own Syrups

One of the simplest bits of alchemy you can perform when mixing drinks at home is making syrups. They are a secret weapon when it comes to creating cocktails. Syrups are like salt for cocktails – they enhance flavours, smooth out the rough edges and take the heat out of spirit-forward drinks.

Making Simple Syrup is the most useful starting point – it's a great all-rounder. Normally it's made with white sugar boiled with water. You can use it in almost any cocktail to add sweetness. If you make your Simple Syrup with other sugars, like demerara, palm or muscovado, you'll have syrups with richer, fudgier flavours. The richer flavours are effective in cocktails with rum, whisky, bourbon or aged tequila.

Infuse a simple syrup with herbs, spices or fruit and you get an instant hit of pure flavour that adds layers of interest to your drinks. Just make sure that any flowers you buy to add to your syrups – whether fresh or dried – are food grade and safe to eat. You don't want to accidentally add something toxic or poisonous to your brews.

Bottle shops and cocktail supply stores sell a huge range of plain and flavoured syrups. For trickier flavours (like pine syrup for the Raider's Gimlet on page 18), it's worth buying ready-made syrups. But if you have a few minutes to spare, these simple-to-make syrups can be easily concocted in your kitchen and will keep well in your fridge.

Simple Syrup

Makes approximately 450ml (16fl oz)

250g (8¾oz) white sugar

250ml (8½fl oz) water

Combine the ingredients in a pan. Set on a medium-high heat and bring to the boil, without stirring. Gently boil for 2 minutes, without stirring. After 2 minutes, take the pan off the heat and let the syrup cool. Funnel the syrup into a sterilised bottle, jar or tub (see below for how to sterilise glass jars and bottles). Seal and store in the fridge for up to 1 month.

Demerara Syrup

Makes approximately 450ml (16fl oz)

250g (8¾oz) demerara sugar

250ml (8½fl oz) water

Combine the ingredients in a pan. Set on a medium-high heat and bring to the boil, without stirring. Gently boil for 2 minutes, without stirring. After 2 minutes, take the pan off the heat and let the syrup cool. Funnel the syrup into a sterilised bottle, jar or tub (see below for how to sterilise glass jars and bottles). Seal and store in the fridge for up to 1 month.

How to Sterilise Glass Jars & Bottles

Preheat your oven to 160°C/Fan 140°C/325°F/Gas Mark 3. Wash the jars, lids and seals and rinse them. Place the jars on a baking tray and slide into the oven and heat for 15 minutes. Take the tray out of the oven and let the jars cool. When they're cool enough to handle, you can add your syrup and seal.

Butterfly Pea Syrup

Makes approximately 450ml (16fl oz)

300ml (10fl oz) water

3 heaped tbsp dried butterfly pea tea flowers

250g (8¾oz) white sugar

Bring the water to the boil. Place the dried butterfly pea tea flowers in a heatproof bowl and pour over the hot water. Set aside to steep for 5 minutes. It should be a deep, rich blue. Strain the tea through a sieve into a pan, gently pressing the flowers to extract any extra liquid.

Put the pan on a high heat and add the sugar. Bring to the boil, without stirring. Gently boil for 2 minutes, without stirring. After 2 minutes, take the pan off the heat and let the syrup cool. Funnel the syrup into a sterilised bottle or jar (see page 11 for how to sterilise glass jars and bottles). Seal and store in the fridge for up to 2 weeks.

Chamomile Syrup

Makes approximately 350ml (12fl oz)

250g (8¾oz) white sugar

250ml (8½fl oz) water

4 heaped tbsp dried chamomile flowers

Combine the sugar and water in a pan. Tip in the dried chamomile flowers. Set on a medium–high heat and bring to the boil, without stirring. Gently boil for 2 minutes, without stirring. After 2 minutes, take the pan off the heat and let the syrup cool.

Once cooled, strain the syrup through a sieve into a bowl and gently press the chamomile flowers to squeeze out any extra liquid. Funnel the syrup into a sterilised bottle or jar (see page 11 for how to sterilise glass jars and bottles). Seal and store in the fridge for up to 2 weeks.

Lavender Syrup

Makes approximately 350ml (12fl oz)

250g (8¾oz) white sugar

250ml (8½fl oz) water

2 tbsp dried lavender flowers

Combine the sugar and water in a pan. Tip in the dried lavender flowers. Set on a medium–high heat and bring to the boil, without stirring. Gently boil for 2 minutes, without stirring. After 2 minutes, take the pan off the heat and let the syrup cool.

Once cooled, strain the syrup through a sieve into a bowl and gently press the lavender flowers to squeeze out any extra liquid. Funnel the syrup into a sterilised bottle or jar (see page 11 for how to sterilise glass jars and bottles). Seal and store in the fridge for up to 2 weeks.

Honey & Chilli Syrup

Makes approximately 400ml (14fl oz)

200g (7oz) runny honey

200ml (7fl oz) water

2 jalapeño or cayenne chillies

Combine the honey and water in a pan. Warm over a medium heat, stirring occasionally, until the liquid starts to boil. Take the liquid off the heat.

Slice the chillies in half and add them to the liquid. Steep for 20 minutes, then taste to see if it's spicy enough for you. If you'd like it hotter, let the syrup steep for another 10 minutes. For a milder syrup, don't slice the chillies. Just add them whole to the syrup for 30 minutes to extract the flavour without the heat.

Discard the chillies. Funnel the syrup into a jar or bottle (see page 11 for how to sterilise glass jars and bottles). Seal and store in the fridge for up to 1 month. If the syrup crystallises, gently warm the syrup to melt before using.

Gins & Vodkas

The fae realms cover all kinds of climates and geographies. Some are snow-slicked winterscapes that smell like pine trees and wood smoke. Others are sun-warmed deserts with hot winds that whip through your hair. But the most popular kind – the realm most likely to lure people in – is lush and green. There the hills roll, the roads are banked by buttercups and daisies and a cool woodland glade is never far away. This gin sour packs all that landscape into one chilled cocktail. It tastes like drinking a meadow. Sweet and herbal, the flavours stay crisp thanks to the fresh lemon juice.

Buttercup

Serves 1

50ml (1¾fl oz) Hendrick's gin

25ml (⅘fl oz) St Germain elderflower liqueur

15ml (½fl oz) fresh lemon juice

15ml (½fl oz) egg white or aquafaba

5ml (⅙fl oz) Chamomile Syrup (see page 12)

Lemon twist, to garnish

Place a coupe glass in the freezer to chill for 5–10 minutes.

Pour the Hendrick's, St Germain, lemon juice, egg white/aquafaba and Chamomile Syrup into a cocktail shaker. Half fill the shaker with ice, seal and shake for 15–30 seconds, or until the tin is frosty.

Strain the cocktail mix into a clean, empty glass. Dump the ice out of your shaker. Then pour the cocktail mix back into the tin. Seal and shake for a further 15–30 seconds, or until the tin feels light.

Take your glass out of the freezer and fine strain the cocktail into the glass. Drop the lemon twist into the glass (see page 9 for how to garnish with a twist) and serve.

If you like the thought of longships cresting the waves and rune-covered warriors running up beaches wielding mighty swords imbued with mystical powers, make this gimlet. It's a cocktail that's long been associated with seafarers. The classic version is made with a mixture of gin and lime cordial. This one includes a ready-made pine syrup, which gives the drink a dash of Scandinavian-forest freshness. There's a hefty double dose of gin because if there's one thing Vikings insist on, it's strong drinks.

Raider's Gimlet

Serves 1

60ml (2fl oz) London dry gin

25ml (⅘fl oz) pine syrup

15ml (½fl oz) fresh lime juice

Lime wheel, to garnish

Place a Nick & Nora glass in the freezer to chill for 5–10 minutes.

Pour the gin, pine syrup and lime juice into a cocktail shaker. Half fill the shaker with ice, seal and shake for 15–30 seconds, or until the tin is frosty.

Take your glass out of the freezer and fine strain the cocktail into the glass. Fix the lime wheel on the rim of the glass and serve.

Dive headfirst into this cool gin sour the same way you'd jump into a lake made of starlight – with cautious enthusiasm and a yelp of delight. It has a subtle floral flavour thanks to the sweet violet liqueur, which also gives the drink a delicate lilac hue. A pinch of silver drink shimmer gives it some sparkle. Sharp and tangy with just enough warmth from the cucumber-scented gin to keep it interesting, it's the perfect summer evening cocktail. One to sip under the stars.

Starlight Pool

Serves 1

50ml (1¾fl oz) Hendrick's gin

15ml (½fl oz) triple sec

15ml (½fl oz) fresh lemon juice

8ml (⅕fl oz) sweet violet liqueur

8ml (⅕fl oz) Simple Syrup (see page 11)

Silver drink shimmer, to garnish

Place a Nick & Nora glass in the freezer to chill for 5–10 minutes.

Pour the gin, triple sec, lemon juice, violet liqueur and Simple Syrup into a cocktail shaker. Half fill the shaker with ice, seal and shake for 15–30 seconds, or until the tin is frosty.

Take the glass out of the freezer and fine strain the cocktail into the glass. Sprinkle a generous pinch of silver drink shimmer into the glass and gently stir. Serve when your drink is glittering.

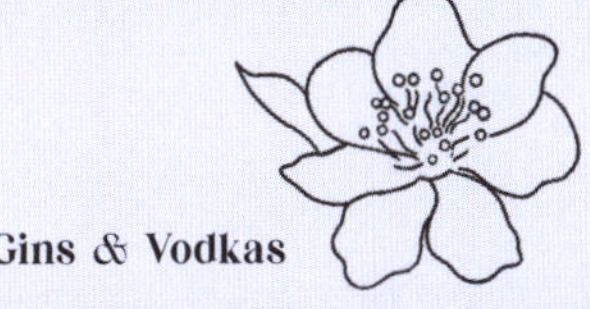

Horse rides that take days and carriage journeys that last weeks are a lot easier to cope with when you can slip into an enchanted sleep. If you've got a fae lord on hand to glamour you into snoozing away the long commute from the mortal world to the faerie realms, then blessed be your gentle dreams. If you don't, try this cocktail instead. It won't make you fall asleep (unless you drink way too many, which isn't advisable) but the calming combination of chamomile, rose and lemon makes it a very relaxing drink. The hefty hit of gin helps too.

Sweet Sleep

Serves 1

50ml (1¾fl oz) Hendrick's gin

20ml (¾fl oz) fresh lemon juice

15ml (½fl oz) rose liqueur

15ml (½fl oz) egg white or aquafaba

8ml (⅕fl oz) Chamomile Syrup (see page 12)

Lemon twist, to garnish

Place a coupe glass in the freezer to chill for 5–10 minutes.

Pour the gin, lemon juice, rose liqueur, egg white/aquafaba and Chamomile Syrup into a cocktail shaker. Half fill the shaker with ice, seal and shake for 15–30 seconds, or until the tin is frosty.

Strain the mix into a clean, empty glass. Dump the ice out of your shaker. Pour the cocktail mix back into the tin. Seal and shake for another 15–30 seconds, or until the tin feels light.

Take your glass out of the freezer and fine strain in the cocktail. Rest the lemon twist (see page 9 for how to garnish with a twist) on the rim of the glass and serve.

The cocktail voted most likely to growl, 'Touch her and you die.' It's a coffee and chocolate twist on a negroni that you wouldn't want to get on the wrong side of, but you'd be drawn to it, nevertheless. Built in the glass, it's easy to mix and you don't need any special equipment to stir it over ice. A barspoon is handy to blend the spirits together, but a normal tablespoon or even the handle of a ladle would work just as well. The mix of gin, Italian amari and coffee liqueur sounds like a tough combo, but it has a soft, chocolatey middle that will make you melt.

Feeling Territorial

Serves 1

15ml (½fl oz) London dry gin

15ml (½fl oz) Campari

15ml (½fl oz) sweet vermouth

15ml (½fl oz) Mr Black Cold Brew Coffee liqueur

3 dashes of chocolate bitters

Grapefruit twist, to garnish

Fill a rocks glass with ice and pour in the gin, Campari, sweet vermouth and coffee liqueur. Dash in the chocolate bitters. Stir them together in the glass for around 30 seconds to chill.

Top up the ice. Express the grapefruit twist over the cocktail (see page 9 for how to express a twist), then drop it into the glass and serve.

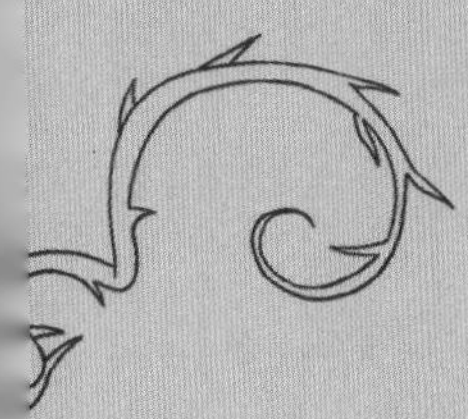

We all have different gifts. Some people can summon lightning so it forks across the sky and crashes into mountain peaks, reducing it all to rubble. Other people are really good at mixing drinks. If you're one of the latter, focus your powers on making this glitter-filled twist on an aviation. A classic gin cocktail that was invented in the early 1900s, aviations are fresh and zesty with a delicate floral flavour thanks to the violet liqueur. This version is sharp enough to jolt your tastebuds awake, then make up for it with a soft, sweet aftertaste.

Storm Warning

Serves 1

35ml (1⅙fl oz) London dry gin

15ml (½fl oz) fresh lime juice

15ml (½fl oz) maraschino liqueur

8ml (⅕fl oz) sweet violet liqueur

8ml (⅕fl oz) Simple Syrup (see page 11)

Silver drink shimmer, to garnish

Place a Nick & Nora glass in the freezer to chill for 5–10 minutes.

Pour the gin, lime juice, maraschino liqueur, violet liqueur and Simple Syrup into a cocktail shaker. Half fill the shaker with ice, seal and shake for 15–30 seconds, or until the tin is frosty.

Take your glass out of the freezer and fine strain the cocktail into the glass. Sprinkle a generous pinch of silver drink shimmer into the glass and gently stir to mix it into the cocktail. Your drink should glitter and shimmer. Serve straight away.

Changeling Ingredients

Drink shimmers come in a range of colours that give your drinks a swirling, glittery appearance. You should be able to find them in cocktail supplies stores. If not, a pinch of edible glitter from the baking aisle in your local supermarket works just as well.

This snow globe–inspired cocktail is a quick way to transport you and a travelling companion to the depths of a biting winter in another realm. For the full woodland effect, prepare the glasses the night before (see Freeze Ahead below for instructions).

Woods In Winter

Serves 2

60ml (2fl oz) vanilla vodka

45ml (1½fl oz) fresh lemon juice

30ml (1fl ox) triple sec

30ml (1fl oz) egg white or aquafaba

25ml (⅘fl oz) Simple Syrup (see page 11)

200ml (7fl oz) soda water, chilled

3 sprigs of rosemary and edible glitter flakes, to garnish

Pour the vanilla vodka, lemon juice, triple sec, egg white/aquafaba and Simple Syrup into a large cocktail shaker. Half fill the tin with ice. Seal and shake for 15–30 seconds, or until the tin is frosty.

Strain the cocktail into a clean, empty large glass. Dump the ice out of the shaker. Pour the cocktail mix back into the tin, seal it and shake again until the tin feels light.

Fill two rocks glasses with ice. Add the rosemary and edible glitter. Fine strain the cocktail into the two glasses. Top each glass up with the chilled soda water. Serve straight away.

Freeze Ahead

Pour enough water into two rocks glasses or balloon glasses to create a 1cm (0.4in) layer in the bottom of the glass. Trim a few rosemary sprigs so they're as tall as the glasses. Strip a few leaves from the base of the sprigs to create tree trunks. Wrap kitchen twine around the rosemary sprigs, then place them in a glass so the 'trunks' are submerged by the water. Wrap the twine around the glass, pulling it tight, to hold the rosemary in place. Tie a knot in the twine and set aside. Repeat with the second glass. Freeze the glasses for at least 2–3 hours, or until the water is frozen solid and the rosemary sprigs are fixed in place. To serve the cocktails, take the glasses out of the freezer and remove the twine. Add a pinch of edible glitter to each glass, then pour in your cocktail mix.

When you're fated to be mated to the alpha, being able to mix a mean martini is an essential life skill. An ice-cold gin cocktail can be very relaxing after a hard day resolving pack disputes, fighting vampires and negotiating with humans. And nothing says social dominance like wielding a barspoon and a mixing glass with great skill. This version is a wet martini, which means it has a high ratio of vermouth to gin. The barspoon of bittersweet Suze liqueur gives it a musky, rasping, fresh-from-the-woods tang. For more ways to tailor the flavours, see Changeling Ingredients below.

Serves 1

10ml (⅓fl oz) dry vermouth

5ml (⅙fl oz) Suze liqueur

55ml (1¾fl oz) London dry gin

2–3 dashes of orange bitters

Lemon twist, to garnish

Place your martini glass in the freezer for 5–10 minutes to chill.

Half fill a mixing glass with ice and pour in the dry vermouth and Suze. Stir a few times to coat the ice, then pour in the gin. Dash in the orange bitters. Stir for a further 30 seconds.

Take the glass out of the freezer and fine strain the Alphatini into the chilled glass. Express the lemon twist over the drink (see page 9 for how to express a twist), then drop it into the glass to garnish. Serve straight away.

Changeling Ingredients
If the Suze is too much werewolf for you, swap it for Velvet Falernum and use celery bitters. It'll make a smoother, sweeter martini with a touch of spice. Consider this version your Betatini.

Fated to be together doesn't always mean you get to stay in the same place or even the same time. Sometimes destiny demands that you split up. In which case you need a drink to mark your last meeting. One with a warm heart – which this drink has, thanks to the gin – and a contrasting combination of flavours to reflect your diverging paths. This cocktail has a mix of tangy lime juice and lush cherry liqueur, which are brought together by the green, herbal notes of the Bénédictine. As fresh as a mountain breeze and as sharp as a forced farewell, it's a beautifully balanced drink.

One Last Look

Serves 2

60ml (2fl oz) London dry gin

40ml (1¼fl oz) D.O.M. Bénédictine liqueur

40ml (1¼fl oz) fresh lime juice

40ml (1¼fl oz) maraschino liqueur

Maraschino cherries, to garnish

Place two coupe glasses in the freezer to chill for 5–10 minutes.

Pour the gin, Bénédictine, lime juice and maraschino liqueur into a large cocktail shaker. Seal and shake for 15–30 seconds, or until the tin is frosty.

Take your glass out of the freezer and fine strain the cocktail into the chilled glasses. Thread the maraschino cherries onto cocktail picks, and rest them on the rims of each glass. Serve straight away.

Of all the elixirs a witch can offer, a Glamour Potion is the most fun – one splash of lemon juice and the drink changes from deep blue to a pretty shade of pink. This drink is strong, so stick to one or two servings of this herbal twist on a lemon drop martini.

Glamour Potion

Serves 1

1 sprig of rosemary

1 sprig of lemon myrtle

50ml (1¾fl oz) lemon vodka

15ml (½fl oz) Butterfly Pea Syrup (see page 12)

10ml (⅓fl oz) triple sec

25ml (⅘fl oz) fresh lemon juice, chilled

Lemon twist, to garnish

Place a martini glass in the freezer to chill for 5–10 minutes.

Put the rosemary and lemon myrtle into a cocktail shaker. Use a muddler or a pestle to crush the herbs until they smell aromatic. Pour in the lemon vodka, Butterfly Pea Syrup and triple sec. Half fill the shaker with ice. Seal and shake well for 15–30 seconds, or until the tin is frosty.

Fine strain the cocktail into your chilled glass. Rest the lemon twist on the rim of the glass (see page 9 for how to garnish with a twist) and serve with the lemon juice in the shot glass on the side.

To drink, pour the lemon juice into the martini and watch it transform. Gently swirl to mix the lemon juice through the cocktail before taking a sip.

Coven-sized Cocktails

Make batches of this cocktail by pouring the lemon vodka, Butterfly Pea Syrup and triple sec into a pitcher (multiply the quantities by the number of servings) and stir to mix. Chill in the fridge for a few hours. When you're ready to serve, bash a few sprigs of rosemary and lemon myrtle together in a pestle and mortar, then add them to the pitcher. Add a few handfuls of ice and stir for 1–2 minutes to chill and dilute. To serve, pour into rocks glasses filled with ice. Give everyone their own shot of lemon juice on the side and let the magic happen.

Elemental beings that can set anything on fire should be terrifying. But somehow, they end up being cute – walking, talking lumps of charcoal that are overcommitted to keeping the hearth warm and the house cosy. If only actual fires showed the same care. Inspired by a sprite's adorable mix of heat and charm, this electric-blue cocktail combines spice with a splash of fizz. A vodka sour lengthened with ginger beer, it gets its colour from blue curaçao and its warmth from a homemade Honey & Chilli Syrup (see page 13). Do not skip the fresh chilli garnish – it's crucial for adding an extra nip of heat.

Fire Sprite

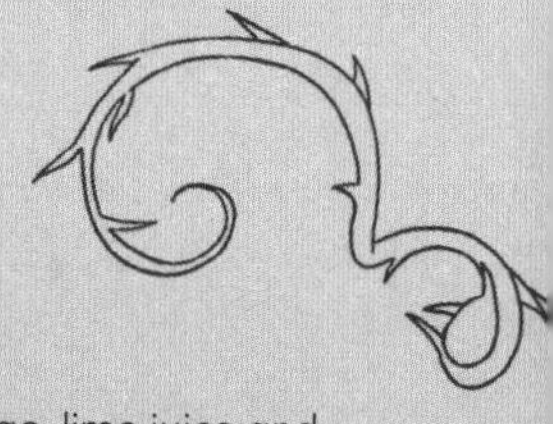

Serves 1

15ml (½fl oz) vodka

15ml (½fl oz) blue curaçao

15ml (½fl oz) fresh lime juice

15ml (½fl oz) Honey & Chilli Syrup (see page 13)

Ginger beer, chilled, to top up

Lime wheel and chilli coins, to garnish

Pour the vodka, blue curaçao, lime juice and Honey & Chilli Syrup into a cocktail shaker. Half fill the shaker with ice, seal and shake for 15–30 seconds, or until the tin is frosty.

Fill an old-fashioned glass with ice cubes. Fine strain the cocktail into the glass. Top up with chilled ginger beer and gently stir to mix.

Tuck the lime wheel into the glass. Add a few chilli coins and serve.

All the best fun happens at night, when moonlight spills across the sky and the world is made of shadow. Midnight meetings seem more clandestine, and adventures are all the more romantic. Combine the dark and light by making this two-toned cocktail, which swirls an inky black layer with a pale dash of creamy booze. Vanilla and spice from the RumChata flows into the tart, coffee-flavoured combination of vodka, Galliano and Mr Black's liqueur, softening the cocktail's more astringent edges. Take this cocktail as proof that the dark needs the light, and vice versa.

Moonlight & Shadows

Serves 1

25ml (⅘fl oz) vodka

15ml (½fl oz) Galliano vanilla liqueur

15ml (½fl oz) Mr Black Cold Brew Coffee liqueur

25ml (⅘fl oz) RumChata cream liqueur

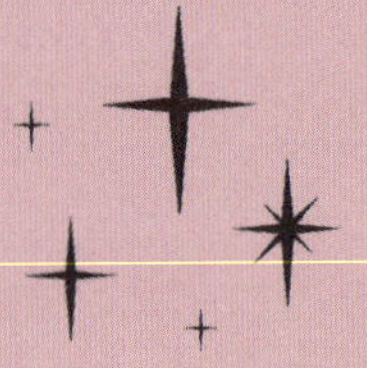

Place a rocks glass in the freezer to chill for 5–10 minutes.

Half fill a mixing glass with ice and pour in the vodka, Galliano and coffee liqueur. Stir together for 30–45 seconds to chill.

Take the rocks glass out of the freezer and fill with ice. Strain the cocktail mix into the glass.

Hold a barspoon in the glass, bowl-side down, and carefully trickle the RumChata over the back of the spoon into the glass. It should slowly sink through the drink, creating swirls of light and dark. Serve straight away, with a drink stirrer so you can mix the layers together.

'Is this what you want?' is the most thrilling line you can ever hear whispered in your ear. That applies whether the offer is the company of a dangerously beautiful, morally complex fae lord or this decadently rich dessert cocktail. The drink is an almost coffee-free version of an espresso martini (there's some cold brew in the coffee liqueur), so if you like espresso martinis but the caffeine content has always caused you problems, this cocktail is your perfect match. The combination of vanilla vodka, Baileys and amaretto gives this drink a mocha-rich sweetness that's indulgently delicious. A drink that's worth saying a vehement yes to.

Enthusiastic Consent

Serves 1

15ml (½fl oz) vanilla vodka

15ml (½fl oz) Baileys Original Irish cream liqueur

15ml (½fl oz) Mr Black Cold Brew Coffee liqueur

15ml (½fl oz) amaretto

15ml (½fl oz) light (pouring) cream

Cocoa powder, to garnish

Place a small coupe glass in the freezer to chill for 5–10 minutes.

Pour the vanilla vodka, Baileys, coffee liqueur, amaretto and cream into a cocktail shaker. Half fill the shaker with ice. Seal and shake vigorously for 15–30 seconds, or until the tin is frosty.

Take your glass out of the freezer and fine strain the cocktail into the chilled glass. Dust over a pinch of cocoa powder to garnish and serve.

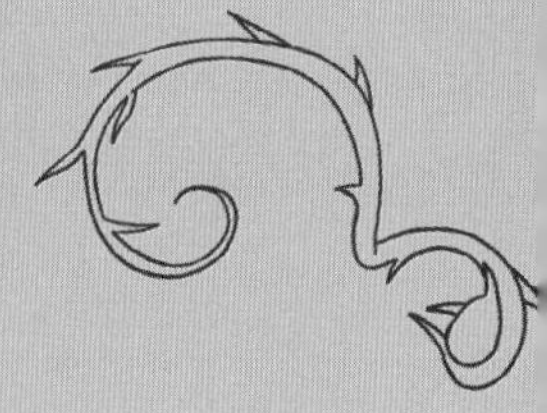

Rums, Tequilas & Bourbons

If you dream of dating a tall, cocky and intense 500-year-old fae warrior who's morally grey, sexily scarred and covered in tattoos, then welcome to the shadow daddy fan club. Though he looks unapproachable and he growls a lot, this brooding bad boy secretly has a sweet heart. Darkly good-looking, with an elegantly balanced bitterness, espresso martinis are basically a shadow daddy in cocktail form. This version has an extra layer of malt from the Guinness, making it an irresistibly smooth drink.

Shadow Daddy

Serves 1

50ml (1¾fl oz) dark rum

25ml (⅘fl oz) hot, fresh espresso

15ml (½fl oz) Mr Black Cold Brew Coffee liqueur

15ml (½fl oz) Guinness

15ml (½fl oz) Demerara Syrup (see page 11)

3 coffee beans, to garnish

Place a coupe glass in the freezer to chill for 5–10 minutes.

Pour the rum, espresso, coffee liqueur, Guinness and Demerara Syrup into a cocktail shaker. Half fill the shaker with ice. Seal and shake vigorously for 30 seconds or until the tin is frosty.

Take your glass out of the freezer and strain the cocktail into the glass. Top with the coffee beans and serve.

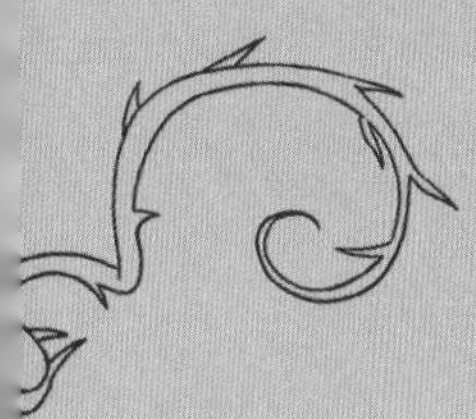

Every brooding MMC needs a smart-mouthed bestie to cheer him up. A boyhood pal who's been with him during the good times and the bad, and who's always armed with a cheeky quip, a charming smile and a dagger. When they kick back with a drink, these great friends deserve something special – like this souped-up mojito. Instead of being lengthened with soda water, it's finished with a generous splash of chilled sparkling white wine, which means this thirst-quenching mint-and-lime cocktail is extra boozy. Perfect for nights when you want to forget all the warfare and focus on getting rowdy with your best mate.

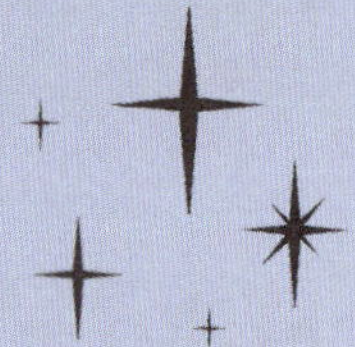

Serves 2

24 fresh mint leaves

1 lime, sliced into 6 wedges

2 tbsp caster (superfine) sugar

120ml (4fl oz) light rum

30ml (1fl oz) fresh lime juice

240ml (8fl oz) dry sparkling white wine, chilled

Rub the rim of two collins glasses with a mint leaf to lightly coat the glasses with the aromatic oils, then drop 12 mint leaves into each glass. Add 2 lime wedges and 1 tbsp caster sugar to each glass. Use a muddler, the end of a rolling pin or a pestle to crush and muddle the mint, lime and sugar together.

Fill each glass with ice. Pour 60ml (2fl oz) rum and 15ml (½fl oz) lime juice into each glass. Stir to mix together.

Top up the drinks with the chilled sparkling white wine. Stir briefly to mix. Drop fresh lime wedges into each glass and serve with reusable straws.

If the fire doesn't get you, the snapping jaws might. Dragons are not to be trifled with, and if they're looking for a fight, the best place to be is hundreds of leagues away. Ideally in a sunshine-soaked bar, enjoying a relaxing blue cocktail that mixes rum with fresh pineapple juice and gives off tropical beach vibes. This turquoise-coloured drink is a riff on a shark attack, a cocktail that's often served with a shot of grenadine in a small shark toy so you can pour it into the drink straight from the shark's mouth. If you can find a small, hollow dragon toy it'd be fun to serve the grenadine in that. If not, a shot glass will do.

Dragon Strike

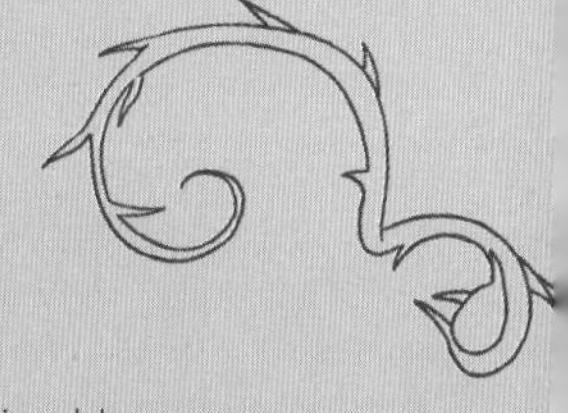

Serves 1

50ml (1¾fl oz) light rum

50ml (1¾fl oz) fresh pineapple juice

15ml (½fl oz) blue curaçao

15ml (½fl oz) fresh lemon juice

15ml (½fl oz) Simple Syrup (see page 11)

15ml (½fl oz) grenadine syrup

Orange wheel and maraschino cherry, to garnish

Pour the rum, pineapple juice, blue curaçao, lemon juice and Simple Syrup into a cocktail shaker. Half fill the shaker with ice. Seal and shake well for 15–30 seconds to chill.

Fill a highball glass with ice and strain in the cocktail mix. Pour the grenadine into a shot glass.

Thread the orange wheel and maraschino cherry onto a cocktail pick and rest it on the rim of the glass. Serve with the shot glass of grenadine on the side.

To drink, pour the grenadine into the glass. It'll swirl down through the drink, looking a little bit like ribbons of blood. Serve with a reusable straw so you can stir the grenadine into the cocktail before you drink.

The first rule of meeting a dragon is to never look it in the eyes. Even if it pulls up very close and puffs hot, steamy breath all over you. Keep your gaze on your feet and be glad you're not getting turned into a scorch mark. If you survive your first encounter with a dragon, go home and immediately recreate the experience by buying a cocktail smoker and making this rum old-fashioned (see page 8 for how to smoke a cocktail). Smooth with a funky touch of sweetness from the Velvet Falernum, it's good served unsmoked. But watching plumes billowing out of a cocktail glass is always a thrill, so it's worth putting in the extra effort.

Dragon's Breath

Serves 1

50ml (1¾fl oz) golden rum

10ml (⅓fl oz) Velvet Falernum

5ml (⅙fl oz) Demerara Syrup (see page 11)

3 dashes of Angostura bitters

Smoke, to garnish

Place an old-fashioned glass in the freezer to chill for 5–10 minutes.

Fill a mixing glass with ice. Pour in the golden rum, Velvet Falernum and Demerara Syrup. Dash in the Angostura bitters. Stir constantly for 45 seconds to 1 minute, until the drink is well chilled.

Take the old-fashioned glass out of the freezer and add a large ice cube (or several smaller cubes). Strain in the cocktail.

Serve just as it is or use a cocktail smoker to smoke the drink and serve it billowing with smoke. Let all the smoke flow out of the glass before taking a sip.

Drinking with vampires can be complicated if you don't want to end up on the bar menu. This blood orange margarita should stop your undead friends from looking thirstily at your neck. The juicy mix of citrus, spicy homemade syrup and a Tajín rim is guaranteed to find favour – who doesn't love a spicy marg? If you'd like to up the heat in this drink, muddle half a chilli in the cocktail shaker before adding all the ingredients and shaking. It'll take your marg's spice rating from a mild and gentle level one to a hot and heavy level five.

SANGARITA

Serves 1

45ml (1½fl oz) silver tequila

25ml (⅘fl oz) triple sec

15ml (½fl oz) blood orange juice

8ml (⅕fl oz) fresh lime juice

8ml (⅕fl oz) Honey & Chilli Syrup (see page 13)

Tajín Clásico seasoning, lime wedge and lime wheel, to garnish

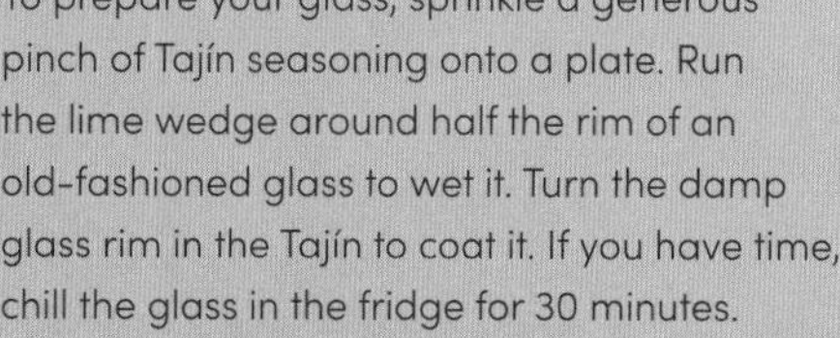

To prepare your glass, sprinkle a generous pinch of Tajín seasoning onto a plate. Run the lime wedge around half the rim of an old-fashioned glass to wet it. Turn the damp glass rim in the Tajín to coat it. If you have time, chill the glass in the fridge for 30 minutes.

Pour the tequila, triple sec, blood orange juice, lime juice and Honey & Chilli Syrup into a cocktail shaker. Half fill the shaker with ice, seal and shake for 15–30 seconds, or until the tin is frosty.

Fill the prepared glass with ice. Fine strain the sangarita into the glass. Tuck in the lime wheel and serve.

When you're on a realm-saving road trip with your annoyingly attractive enemy, there's nothing worse than arriving at the local inn, only to find that there's just one room left. It's always an awkwardly sized double bed tucked into a tiny attic with no option but to snuggle. Nightmare. If forced proximity is your kink, then you'll love both the shared straw mattress under the eaves and this frozen margarita. It's a silky mix of citrus and agave, and it gets its pretty lilac colour from the Butterfly Pea Syrup. Made for two but served in one glass, you'll have to get *very* close to the person you're sharing it with to drink.

Just One Glass

Serves 2

90ml (3fl oz) silver tequila

60ml (2fl oz) triple sec

50ml (1¾fl oz) fresh lime juice

60ml (2fl oz) Butterfly Pea Syrup (see page 12)

Edible flowers, to garnish

Place a large hurricane glass in the freezer to chill for 5–10 minutes.

Pour the tequila, triple sec, lime juice and Butterfly Pea Syrup into a high-speed blender. Add 400g (14oz) ice to the blender. Blitz on high speed for 30 seconds to 1 minute, until the margarita mix is slushy.

Take the chilled glass out of the freezer. Pour the slushy cocktail mix into the glass. Add two reusable straws and garnish with a few edible flowers. Find someone to share it with and drink.

It's always the folk with green eyes that get you into trouble: a dragon rider with an emerald-bright stare; a fae lord whose forest-green irises are flecked with gold; or a wood witch who sizes you up with one mossy glance. Hold tight and hope that the adventure they take you on is as much fun as this fizzy, frothy cocktail.

Make Me Shiver

Serves 1

30ml (1fl oz) light rum

30ml (1fl oz) Midori liqueur

30ml (1fl oz) fresh lime juice

25ml (⅘fl oz) light (pouring) cream

15ml (½fl oz) Simple Syrup (see page 11)

15ml (½fl oz) egg white or aquafaba

100ml (3½fl oz) soda water, chilled

Place a collins glass in the freezer to chill for 5–10 minutes.

Pour the rum, Midori, lime juice, cream, Simple Syrup and egg white/aquafaba into a cocktail shaker. Half fill the shaker with ice. Seal and shake vigorously for 30 seconds, or until the tin is frosty.

Strain the mix into a clean, empty glass. Dump the ice out of your shaker. Pour the cocktail mix back into the shaker. Seal and shake for another 15–30 seconds, or until the tin feels light.

Take your glass out of the freezer. Hold the cocktail shaker in your dominant hand and the soda water bottle in your other hand. Make sure the cocktail shaker has a strainer fitted. Slowly pour three-quarters of the cocktail into the chilled glass while simultaneously trickling in chilled soda water. Once you've poured three-quarters of the cocktail into the glass, stop. Let the drink settle for 1–2 minutes, then top it up with the remaining cocktail mix from the shaker and a splash more soda water.

Serve straight away.

When he knocks at the bedchamber door, the armoire trembles, knowing what happened to the last three armoires. The same goes for the desk, chair, bedside table and lamp. All splintered into matchsticks because some people can't control themselves in bed. It's a shame for the furniture, though good news for the village carpenter who has developed a lucrative line in replacement household goods. If you're feeling feral, save the sideboard and mix this drink instead. Fragrant with lemon and fennel, it has a lip-tingling twist of absinthe and is warmed by a hit of brandy. Savagely good.

Beast in the Sheets

Serves 1

20ml (¾fl oz) brandy

20ml (¾fl oz) triple sec

20ml (¾fl oz) light rum

5ml (⅙fl oz) fresh lemon juice

5ml (⅙fl oz) Simple Syrup (see page 11)

5ml (⅙fl oz) absinthe

Lemon twist, to garnish

Place a Nick & Nora glass in the freezer to chill for 5–10 minutes.

Pour the brandy, triple sec, rum, lemon juice and Simple Syrup into a cocktail shaker. Half fill the shaker with ice, seal and shake for 15–30 seconds, or until the tin is frosty.

Take your glass out of the freezer. Add a barspoon of absinthe and turn the glass to coat the inside with the absinthe. Tip out any excess.

Fine strain the cocktail into the glass. Express the lemon twist over the cocktail (see page 9 for how to express a twist), then drop it into the glass and serve.

This cocktail may have a modest blush to it, but our bold FMC doesn't when she's stripping off for a swim, a change of ballgowns or a post-battle medical exam. Good for her. Let there be more shameless stripping off (in socially acceptable scenarios) and more body confidence all round. To celebrate our newfound immodesty, make this twist on a naked and famous. It tastes just like biting into a grapefruit – skin, pith and juice. Zingy and moreish.

Naked & Shameless

Serves 1

20ml (¾fl oz) reposado tequila

20ml (¾fl oz) Campari

20ml (¾fl oz) Galliano vanilla liqueur

20ml (¾fl oz) fresh lime juice

Lime twist, to garnish

Place a small coupe glass in the freezer to chill for 5–10 minutes.

Pour the tequila, Campari, Galliano and lime juice into a cocktail shaker and half fill it with ice. Seal and shake well for 15–30 seconds, or until the tin is frosty.

Take your glass out of the freezer and fine strain the cocktail into the glass. Rest the lime twist on the rim of the glass (see page 9 for how to garnish with a twist) and serve.

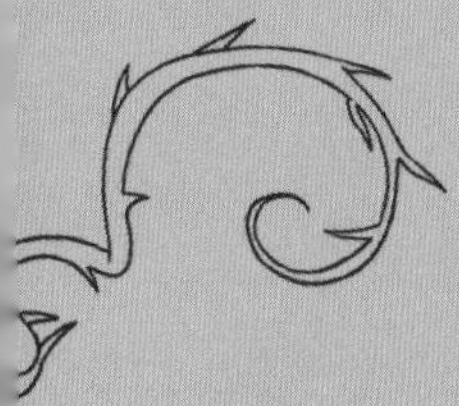

We've all been there: forced to choose between living the life we've always dreamed of or ending a centuries-old war by marrying the square-jawed, broad-shouldered, super-annoying son of our enemy. With the lives of so many people on the line, there's nothing else to do but get trussed up in an elaborate wedding dress and calm any pre-marriage jitters with a stiff drink. A flower-scented twist on a daiquiri seems like an appropriate choice for a wedding breakfast. This version is tangy and sharp, with a prickle of boozy heat from the rum. The Lavender Syrup mellows out the flavours and folds in a reassuring note of calm.

Marriage Pact

Serves 1

50ml (1¾fl oz) golden rum

15ml (½fl oz) fresh lime juice

15ml (½fl oz) Lavender Syrup (see page 13)

Lime wheel, to garnish

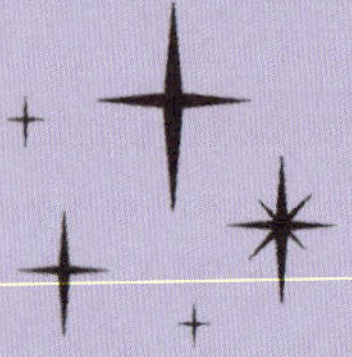

Place a Nick & Nora glass in the freezer to chill for 5–10 minutes.

Pour the rum, lime juice and Lavender Syrup into a cocktail shaker. Half fill the shaker with ice, seal and shake for 15–30 seconds, or until the tin is frosty.

Take your glass out of the freezer and fine strain the cocktail into the glass. Fix the lime wheel on the rim of the glass and serve.

If you're fed up waiting for a sacred pair bond to snap into place, give destiny a shove by mixing up a batch of passion fruit margaritas. In the unlikely event that the cocktail doesn't draw in your destined lover, you'll still have a margarita to drink, so there's no bad outcomes here. This passion fruit marg is made with reposado tequila, which is rested for between two months and a year in oak barrels. The tequila's savoury richness opens up the luscious flavours in the passion fruit liqueur. Add a crisp splash of lime juice and a dash of spicy syrup, and you get a cocktail that's fresh, full-bodied and full of warmth.

Fated Mates

Serves 2

90ml (3fl oz) reposado tequila

50ml 1¾fl oz) passion fruit liqueur

30ml (1fl oz) fresh lime juice

20ml (¾fl oz) Honey & Chilli Syrup (see page 13)

Lime wheels, to garnish

Pour the tequila, passion fruit liqueur, lime juice and Honey & Chilli Syrup into a large cocktail shaker. Half fill the shaker with ice, seal and shake for 15–30 seconds, or until the tin is frosty.

Fill two rocks glasses with crushed ice. Strain the cocktail into the glasses. Fix a lime wheel on the rim of each glass and serve straight away.

If your tastes lean more towards the bazaars of Old Cairo and skimming over hot Saharan sands in the company of an infuriatingly handsome djinni, then this cocktail is for you. The mix of bourbon, lime juice and butterscotch schnapps is fudgy and fruity – similar to the sweet date wines that have been the downfall of many a lovelorn, lamp-dwelling desert spirit. Smoking the cocktail evokes the hot, burning sands and the fug of the souk (see page 8 for how to smoke a cocktail). Crisp with a twist of sugar and spice, this thirst-quenching long drink will help take the heat out of the day – if not your heart.

Desert Kiss

Serves 1

60ml (2fl oz) bourbon

30ml (1fl oz) fresh lime juice

15ml (½fl oz) butterscotch schnapps

50ml (1¾fl oz) ginger beer, chilled

Smoke, to garnish

Pour the bourbon, lime juice and butterscotch schnapps into a cocktail shaker. Half fill the shaker with ice. Seal and shake well for 15–30 seconds, or until the tin is frosty.

Half fill a highball glass with ice and strain in the cocktail mix. Top up the glass with the ginger beer, leaving a small gap. Gently stir to mix.

Use a smoke lid to smoke the cocktail for 30 seconds.

Serve with smoke billowing out of the glass and with a reusable straw to stir it all together. Let the smoke flow out of the glass before taking a sip.

Whiskies & Liqueurs

One moment you're sitting around the dinner table in your humble cottage with your loving family. The next moment you've been kidnapped by a supernatural being and whisked away to a magical realm. When you wake up in your chamber the next day, you notice two things: how warm and comfortable a feather bed can be and that the skies outside your bedroom window don't look that familiar. In fact, they're distinctly odd. This retro cocktail recreates that otherworldly horizon with three brightly coloured layers: a red, grenadine-rich base, a refreshing citrus middle and a pale green layer of Midori and vodka on top. It tastes like a sweetshop pick'n'mix.

Strange Skies

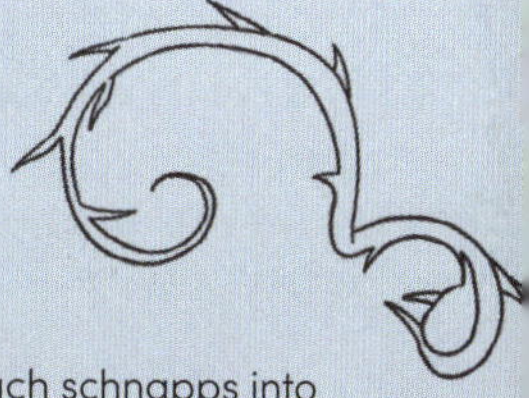

Serves 1

25ml (⅘fl oz) grenadine syrup

25ml (⅘fl oz) peach schnapps

50ml (1¾fl oz) orange juice

8ml (⅕fl oz) fresh lime juice

10ml (⅓fl oz) cold water

10ml (⅓fl oz) Midori liqueur

20ml (¾fl oz) vodka

Orange wheel and maraschino cherry, to garnish

Pour the grenadine and peach schnapps into a collins glass and stir them together. Add enough ice to the collins glass to fill it.

Pour the orange juice and lime juice into a separate mixing glass. Half fill it with ice and stir for around 30 seconds to chill the fruit juice. Strain slowly into the collins glass – the orange layer should float above the grenadine layer.

In a separate, clean glass, mix together the water, Midori and vodka. Pour it over the back of your barspoon into the collins glass, so the green Midori layers floats above the orange layer (see page 8 for how to layer a drink).

Thread the orange wheel and maraschino cherry onto a pick and rest it on the glass. Serve straight away.

All it takes is one unguarded look and you're caught in a Vampire's Thrall – hypnotised by those magnetic eyes that all vampires seem to have. The things those lethally handsome members of the undead could force you to do are too terrible to contemplate. Which is why it's best to keep your eyes averted whenever you're near vampire territory. Unless that sort of thing interests you? In which case, no judgement here. Just a deceptively sweet cocktail that lures you in with its jammy, raspberry pie flavours before hitting you with a fiery hit of booze. A layered shot (see page 8 for how to layer a drink), it's more dangerous than it looks.

Vampire's Thrall

Serves 1

10ml (⅓fl oz) raspberry liqueur

10ml (⅓fl oz) amaretto

10ml (⅓fl oz) vanilla vodka

Raspberries (optional), to garnish

A few hours before you want to make your shots, put all the liquors in the fridge to chill.

To make a shot, pour the chilled raspberry liqueur into a large shot glass. Hold a barspoon in the glass, bowl-side down, and slowly pour the amaretto over the back of the spoon to float the liquid on top of the raspberry liqueur. Then do the same with the vanilla vodka, so it floats on top.

Drink straight away. You can either down it in one (being sure to drink sensibly) or stir to mix the spirits together and serve.

If you'd like a longer drink, double the quantities and serve in a rocks glass. Garnish with fresh raspberries and drink straight away.

Never underestimate what a short, weedy-looking woman can do. She might seem breakable, but if she's powered by grit and rage, then she's a formidable foe – especially if she has a cohort of friends ready to step in and defend her honour. Add in enough book-learning to make up for her lack of physical strength, and you're the one who could end up in trouble. Similarly, don't get too casual when it comes to knocking back this shot. It might not look like much, but the combination of spirits is potent. Sweet at first, the peppery heat from the rye whiskey has enough of a kick to make its presence felt.

Small But Mighty

Serves 1

5ml (⅙fl oz) D.O.M. Bénédictine liqueur

15ml (½fl oz) sweet vermouth

10ml (⅓fl oz) rye whiskey

A few hours before you want to make your shots, put all the liquors in the fridge to chill.

To make a shot, pour the chilled Bénédictine, sweet vermouth and whiskey into a large shot glass. Drink straight away. You can sip it or knock it back in one go (remembering the warning about how mighty this shot can be).

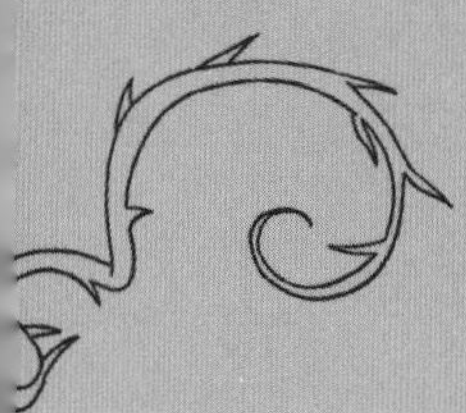

She's a 10, but she's a weresnake – so she's an 11? Supple, seductive and not prepared to share, snake girls and lamias are not to be tangled with. They'll lure you in, promising that they just want to talk. But once you're caught up in their soft, silky coils, you're not getting out. So stay sharp, because their sweet words are as beguiling as this smooth and creamy shot. A velvety mix of Baileys and chocolate liqueur, it looks like a harmless little drink. By the time the heat from the brandy hits, you'll realise too late that this tiny cocktail has teeth.

Serpent's Smile

Serves 1

10ml (⅓fl oz) white crème de cacao

15ml (½fl oz) Baileys Original Irish cream liqueur

5ml (⅙fl oz) brandy

A few hours before you want to make your shots, put all the liquors in the fridge to chill.

To make a shot, pour the chilled crème de cacao into a large shot glass. Add the Baileys, then the brandy. Drink straight away in one mouthful, and follow it with something hydrating.

If you're not keen on being visited by the fae, then you need to ward your home. Hanging iron charms and ash twigs outside your house should stop the fair folk calling by, but if you can't get your hands on either of those, try making a cocktail inspired by those protective elements instead. This juicy riff on a blood and sand cocktail has a hint of bitterness and smoke hiding beneath the fruit. Use a good-quality sweet vermouth to add an extra layer of herbs and berries to the drink.

Iron & Ash

Serves 1

25ml ($\frac{4}{5}$fl oz) blended Scotch whisky

25ml ($\frac{4}{5}$fl oz) sweet vermouth, such as Punt e Mes

25ml ($\frac{4}{5}$fl oz) fresh ruby grapefruit juice

25ml ($\frac{4}{5}$fl oz) Ferro-China aperitif liqueur

3 dashes of black walnut bitters

Grapefruit twist, to garnish

Place a small coupe glass in the freezer to chill for 5–10 minutes.

Pour the whisky, vermouth, grapefruit juice and Ferro-China into a cocktail shaker. Dash in the black walnut bitters. Half fill the shaker with ice, seal and shake for 15–30 seconds, or until the tin is frosty.

Fine strain the cocktail into the chilled coupe. Express the grapefruit twist over the drink (see page 9 for how to express a twist) then drop it into the glass and serve.

Changeling Ingredients

Ferro-China liqueurs are a type of sweet Italian aperitif that have a citrussy, floral flavour. They have iron citrate added to them, which is ideal for adding a hint of iron to cocktails, especially if they're combined with black walnut bitters. Baliva and Bisleri are the leading brands. If you can't find them, swap in Averna Amaro and use chocolate bitters instead.

Not everyone wants to date the menacing MMC with black hair, perfect abs and rage issues. Some people prefer a sweet-natured blond with golden retriever energy (and also great abs). This cocktail is for them. Fresh, fizzy and lower in alcohol, it's an easy-going drink even though it's made with a bitter aperitif. The Suze liqueur, which gets its mouth-puckering flavour from gentian root, is sweetened with a generous measure of lemonade. You still get the funky, straw-and-herb hit of the Suze, but it's eased by the citrus and sugar. All the faerie magic with none of the dark consequences.

Tall, Blond & Handsome

Serves 1

35ml (1⅙fl oz) Suze liqueur

15ml (½fl oz) fresh lemon juice

150ml (5fl oz) sparkling lemonade, chilled

Lemon wheel, to garnish

Fill a highball glass with ice. Pour in the Suze and lemon juice. Stir to mix.

Top up the glass with the chilled lemonade. Stir briefly to mix. Tuck the lemon wheel into the glass and serve with a reusable straw.

A responsible shadow daddy always drinks his contraceptive potion, even if it is herbal and bitter. Nothing gets in the way of saving the realm more than having to find affordable childcare. Absinthe has been added to this alcoholic – and very non-effective – version of a contraceptive shot. Traditional absinthes have a mouth-puckering bitterness to them due to the wormwood, as well as a heavy dose of aniseed and fennel. A little goes a long way. Combined with Galliano and Cointreau, it makes a short cocktail that tastes like old-fashioned liquorice sweets.

Dom Shot

Serves 1

15ml (½fl oz) Galliano vanilla liqueur

15ml (½fl oz) Cointreau orange liqueur

5ml (⅙fl oz) absinthe

A few hours before you want to make your shots, put all the liquors in the fridge to chill.

To make a shot, measure the chilled Galliano, Cointreau and absinthe into a large shot glass. Drink straight away.

If you like liquorice, this is nice sipped – especially with coffee after a meal. If not, then you'll probably prefer to knock this shot back in one go and follow it up with something sweet and refreshing, like For Your Own Good (see page 105). The cola spices and pomegranate would be a nice chaser for the absinthe.

A flash of fangs when he smiles and the salty taste of blood when he kisses you means one thing: you're dating a vampire. What he wants to taste is *you*. If intense is your vibe for both romance and drinks, then this darkly bitter cocktail is it. The Ferro-China adds a metallic roughness, while the Campari and Averna Amaro mix in a sharp green and earthy blend of herb stems and roots. Imagine a negroni with more bite.

Bite My Lip

Serves 1

25ml (⅘fl oz) Ferro-China aperitif liqueur

25ml (⅘fl oz) Campari

25ml (⅘fl oz) Averna Amaro

Orange wheel, to garnish

Fill an old-fashioned glass with ice and pour in the Ferro-China, Campari and Averna Amaro. Use a barspoon to stir them together for around 30 seconds to chill.

Top up the ice. Tuck the orange wheel into the glass and serve.

Changeling Ingredients

If you can't find Ferro-China, make this twist on a negroni with a sweet vermouth, like Punt e Mes, instead. It'll be bitter and jammy but not as mouth-puckeringly metallic. If you'd like to ease off on the bitterness, swap the Ferro-China for London dry gin. It will taste more like a standard negroni but with a drop more bitterness, thanks to the Averna Amaro. For a guide to Ferro-China, go to page 79.

The most romantic place in the world is a rose garden in the early evening, when the air is heavy with the sweet scent of flowers. You can trade longing glances with your forbidden love, indulge in a first kiss or even pluck up the courage to propose marriage. Turning that picture-perfect location into a cocktail isn't just about capturing the Turkish delight flavours of a rose but adding in the lavishness of the whole garden. Luckily, there's chocolate liqueurs that can do that. Combine with a dash of sour pomegranate juice and a spoonful of musky Velvet Falernum, and you get a bright pink drink with a lusciously botanical flavour. For the perfect serve, make your own edible rose garnish with a strip of apple peel and mint leaves.

Kiss in a Rose Garden

Serves 1

25ml (⅘fl oz) white crème de cacao

25ml (⅘fl oz) pomegranate juice

10ml (⅓fl oz) rose liqueur

15ml (½fl oz) Velvet Falernum

Red-skinned apple, lemon juice and 2 mint leaves, to garnish

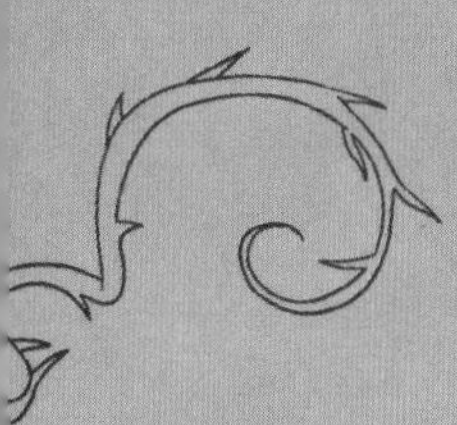

Place a Nick & Nora glass in the freezer to chill for 5–10 minutes.

Make the garnish by peeling a long strip from the apple. Lay it, white side up, on your chopping board and squeeze a little lemon juice over it. Then roll it up loosely to make a rose shape. Thread it onto a cocktail pick with the mint leaves. Set aside for later.

Pour the white crème de cacao, the pomegranate juice, rose liqueur and Velvet Falernum into a cocktail shaker. Half fill the shaker with ice. Seal and shake well for 15–30 seconds, or until the tin is frosty.

Take your glass out of the freezer and fine strain the cocktail into the glass. Rest the garnish on the rim of the glass and serve.

Awakening the dormant, infernal magics within can be tricky – unless you know how to make a wicked espresso martini. In which case, you have a shortcut to trouble. A cocktail that brings out the wild side in the sweetest of folks, this classic espresso martini is made with vanilla vodka, fresh espresso and coffee liqueur. It includes a shot of stickily sweet amaretto and a few dashes of chocolate bitters to draw out the cocktail's rich, nutty flavours. Smooth with a hint of mocha, it's dangerously easy to drink. Proceed with caution.

Dark Magic

Serves 1

25ml (⅘fl oz) amaretto

25ml (⅘fl oz) vanilla vodka

25ml (⅘fl oz) hot, fresh espresso

25ml (⅘fl oz) Mr Black Cold Brew Coffee liqueur

3 dashes of chocolate bitters

Cocoa powder, to garnish

Put a coupe glass into the freezer to chill for 5–10 minutes.

Pour the amaretto, vanilla vodka, espresso and coffee liqueur into a cocktail shaker. Dash in the chocolate bitters. Half fill the shaker with ice. Seal and shake vigorously for 15–30 seconds, or until the tin is frosty.

Take your glass out of the freezer and fine strain the cocktail into the glass. Dust over a pinch of cocoa powder to garnish. Serve straight away.

If I've learned one thing from reading romantasy novels, it's that when men experience any strong emotion, they flex their jaw. No wonder their jawlines are so sharp. Bottling up emotions is a very masculine pastime, and it needs an equally manly cocktail to go with it. Nothing fits the bill better than a Manhattan. This is a version of a 'perfect' Manhattan, but made with blended Scotch whisky that's balanced with a mix of sweet vermouth and Bénédictine. Boozy, woody and aromatic, it's ideal drunk by a log fire with a leather-bound book on your lap and someone frustrating on your mind.

Serves 1

60ml (2fl oz) blended Scotch whisky

15ml (½fl oz) sweet vermouth

15ml (½fl oz) D.O.M. Bénédictine liqueur

3 dashes of orange bitters

Lemon wheel and maraschino cherry, to garnish

Place a small coupe glass in the freezer to chill for 5–10 minutes.

Fill a mixing glass with ice. Pour in the whisky, vermouth and Bénédictine. Dash in the orange bitters. Stir until well chilled – around 1 minute.

Take your glass out of the freezer and strain the cocktail into the glass. Thread the lemon wheel and maraschino cherry onto a cocktail pick and balance it on the rim of the glass. Serve straight away.

If enemy, why lover shaped? In particular, why lover *scented*? Fresh mint, citrus, a hint of leather and wood – it's a heady combination. The minute that aftershave companies translate that mix into a cologne, we'll all be in trouble. While we wait, make this whiskey smash. The mint and lemon are muddled together to release their aromas. Then rye whiskey and black walnut bitters are added, giving the cocktail a masculine whiff of oak barrels, earthy walnuts and cola spices. The sharpness of the citrus dampens down the whiskey's sweeter elements, so you get more of the alcohol's heat and roughness. You'll need plenty of ice to cool the drink – and yourself – down.

Love My Enemy

Serves 1

15ml (½fl oz) Simple Syrup (see page 11)

15ml (½fl oz) fresh lemon juice

5 large fresh mint leaves

60ml (2fl oz) rye whiskey

4 dashes of black walnut bitters

Lemon wheel and mint sprigs, to garnish

Pour the Simple Syrup and lemon juice into a cocktail shaker. Add the mint leaves. Muddle them together to bruise the mint so it releases its aroma.

Half fill the shaker with ice and pour in the whiskey. Dash in the black walnut bitters. Seal and shake well for around 30 seconds, or until the tin is frosty.

Fill an old-fashioned glass with crushed ice and strain in the cocktail. Tuck the lemon wheel and a couple of small mint sprigs into the glass. Serve with a reusable straw.

Changeling Ingredients

If you can't find black walnut bitters, swap in Angostura bitters. It'll give this cocktail an aromatic dash of spice.

A noble hero who'd sacrifice himself for you is an attractive prospect. But a villain who'd lay waste to the entire world just for you? Irresistible. It's the hint of danger that keeps you hooked. In the same way, the fiery splash of whiskey in this cocktail makes you slow down and appreciate every sip. The whiskey is shaken with Cynar, an Italian amaro flavoured with artichokes. It gives the drink a throat-catching bitterness that seems hard to like at first but quickly becomes addictive. If you prefer your villains easier on the approach, swap it for Averna Amaro and enjoy a richer, more chocolatey cocktail.

Villain Gets the Girl

Serves 1

60ml (2fl oz) rye whiskey

25ml (⅘fl oz) Cynar aperitif

3 dashes of black walnut bitters

Maraschino cherry, to garnish

Place a small coupe glass in the freezer to chill for 5–10 minutes.

Fill a mixing glass with ice. Pour in the whiskey and Cynar. Dash in the black walnut bitters. Stir until well chilled – around 1 minute.

Take your glass out of the freezer and strain the cocktail into the glass. Drop in the maraschino cherry to garnish and serve.

Changeling Ingredients

Nutty and woody with a tart dose of spice, black walnut bitters go really well with whiskey, bourbon and rum cocktails. They bring out the liquors' richness and can turn smoky with a bittersweet Italian amaro in the mix. If you can't find them, try swapping in chocolate bitters (smoother and sweeter) or coffee bitters (smoky and dark).

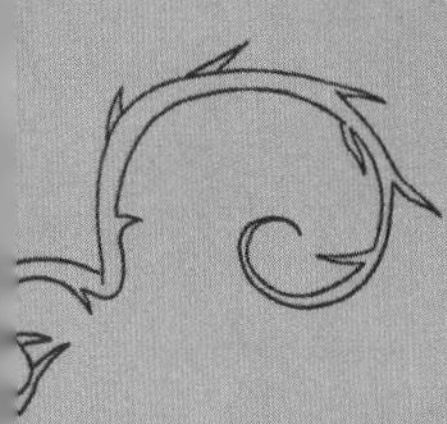

How much damage can one kiss do? It's just a kiss – it's not like it'll lead to an unbreakable mate bond or reveal magical powers you didn't know you had. Right? For those resisting a pash with a fae prince, this luscious dessert cocktail is a good distraction. Velvety-rich with hints of marshmallow and ice cream, it gets it's indulgent flavour from RumChata, a liqueur that blends rum with cream, sugar, cinnamon and aromatic spices.

Forbidden Kiss

Serves 1

25ml (⅘fl oz) vanilla vodka

25ml (⅘fl oz) RumChata cream liqueur

25ml (⅘fl oz) butterscotch schnapps

Salted caramel sauce, to garnish

Place a martini glass in the freezer to chill for 5–10 minutes.

Pour the vanilla vodka, RumChata and butterscotch schnapps into a cocktail shaker. Half fill the shaker with ice, seal and shake for 15–30 seconds, or until the tin is frosty.

Take the martini glass out of the freezer. Hold the glass at a 45-degree angle and drizzle salted caramel sauce in it, turning the glass as you go. Fine strain the cocktail into the glass. Serve straight away.

ZERO-PROOF

Any healer knows that lavender is good for calming nerves, soothing anxieties and relieving stress. Turn the flower into a restorative tonic by adding it to fresh lemon juice and sparkling water. The secret to a good Lavender Lemonade is to make your own Lavender Syrup (see page 13). Tangy, floral and not too sweet, sip this flower-scented non-alcoholic drink all day long. Make it an alcoholic drink by adding a shot of vodka.

Lavender Lemonade

Serves 1

35ml (1⅙fl oz) Lavender Syrup (see page 13)

25ml (⅘fl oz) fresh lemon juice

150ml (5fl oz) sparkling water, chilled

Flower Ice Cubes (see right), to garnish

Fill a highball glass with Flower Ice Cubes. Pour in the Lavender Syrup and lemon juice, and gently stir to mix.

Top up with the chilled sparkling water. Stir a couple of times, then serve with a reusable straw.

How to Make Flower Ice Cubes

Ice cubes with edible flowers suspended in the middle look gorgeous. They take a few days' prep, but most of it is freezer time.

To make them, boil a kettle of water and let it cool. Half fill an ice cube tray with the water. Add 1–2 edible flowers to each cube. Freeze overnight. The next day, top up the tray with more cooled, boiled water. Freeze again for 8–12 hours, until the ice cubes are solid.

Good flowers to use in ice cubes include violas, pansies, linaria, dianthus and herb flowers. Make sure the flowers you buy are grown for eating and not for display.

When you've survived an attack by dark-magic wielders and your on/off fae love interest is refusing to talk about it, retreat to your bedchamber with your cheerful house sprite and share warming mugs of hot chocolate. This luxurious version is made with a mix of dark and milk chocolate, plus the most mood stabilising and comforting of all the instant drink powders: Milo. It'll soothe your nerves and give you time to brood in peace – nothing too bad can happen when you've got a mugful of Milo. Especially when it's topped with plenty of whipped cream.

Malted Molten Hot Chocolate

Serves 2

75g (2½oz) dark chocolate, around 80% cocoa solids

75g (2½oz) milk chocolate

6 tbsp Milo powder

2 tbsp soft brown sugar

600ml (20fl oz) full-cream (whole) milk

100ml (3½fl oz) thickened (heavy) cream

Whipped cream and Milo powder, to garnish

Roughly chop the dark and milk chocolate, and place into a small pan. Add the Milo and soft brown sugar.

Pour in the milk and cream. Set the pan on a medium heat and gently warm, whisking constantly, until the chocolate has melted and is smoothly combined.

Ladle the hot chocolate into two heatproof glasses or mugs. Top with whipped cream and dust over a little Milo to garnish.

If you're feeling overprotective, mix up a batch of this mocktail and demand all your friends start their night with a glass of lightly sparkling fruit punch. If they complain and insist they don't need babysitting, tell them it's for their own good and then make them drink a second round. Tonight, you're everyone's bodyguard – whether they like it or not. At least the drink is delicious. The pomegranate juice adds a dry crispness to the sweet cola, while the fruit is a good match with the spices. If you want a drink that is completely alcohol-free, leave out the Angostura bitters.

For Your Own Good

Serves 4

480ml (16¾fl oz) pomegranate juice, chilled

480ml (16¾fl oz) cola, chilled

18 dashes of Angostura bitters

Orange wheels, to garnish

Half fill a pitcher with ice. Pour in the chilled pomegranate juice. Top up with the chilled cola.

Dash in the Angostura bitters and gently stir to mix.

Serve in collins glasses with extra ice. Tuck an orange wheel into each glass just before serving.

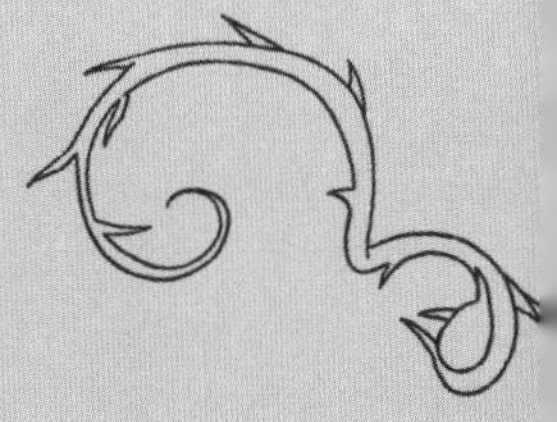

Being queen of the underworld has its challenges. Not the least of which is being forced to marry the god who kidnapped you and then spending six months of the year shut away from the sunshine and ruling over the dead by his side. You can understand why Persephone might shed the occasional, regretful tear. The bitterness of her situation flavours this zero-proof mocktail. Along with crisp, sweet pomegranate juice, it's a rich, royal colour – as befits an immortal queen – with a hint of fizz from the soda water. It's not much comfort, but until Hades agrees to go to marriage counselling, it'll have to do.

Persephone's Tears

Serves 1

150ml (5fl oz) pomegranate juice

25ml (⅘fl oz) bitter concentrate syrup

Soda water, chilled, to top up

Pomegranate seeds and lemon wheel, to garnish

Fill a collins glass with ice. Pour in the pomegranate juice and bitter concentrate. Gently stir to mix.

Add more ice to the glass to fill it back up, if you need to. Top up with chilled soda water. Stir a couple of times to mix. Sprinkle a few pinches of pomegranate seeds over the top of the drink and tuck in the lemon wheel. Serve with a reusable straw.

Changeling Ingredients

Bitter concentrate is a ruby-red syrup that tastes like Campari and Aperol, but without the alcohol. It pairs well with red-fruit juices, like pomegranate and cranberry. If you're not keen on adding a hint of bitterness to your mocktail, try blood orange syrup, hibiscus syrup or grenadine instead.

He's a 900-year-old fae warrior with a reputation for going berserk on the battlefield. She's a 19-year-old human who hangs out in libraries and has something to prove. Of course they've got loads in common and are extremely compatible: there's the emotional immaturity, poor communication skills and their shared tendency to run headfirst into danger with no consideration for the consequences. When this level of recklessness is present, it's best if the bonded pair stay off the booze and stick to a safe, sweet and sticky mocktail, like this fruit-flavoured alcohol-free drink. That way, all the bad decisions are their own.

Problematic Age Gap

Serves 1

25ml (⅘fl oz) grenadine syrup

75ml (2½fl oz) fresh orange juice

8ml (⅕fl oz) fresh lime juice

125ml (4¼fl oz) sparkling lemonade, chilled

Orange wheel and maraschino cherry, to garnish

Pour the grenadine into a hurricane glass. Fill the glass with ice cubes.

In a separate glass, combine the orange juice and lime juice. Slowly pour them into the hurricane glass. They should float above the grenadine. Top up the glass with the chilled lemonade.

Thread the orange wheel and maraschino cherry onto a cocktail pick, and rest it on the rim of the glass. Serve with a reusable straw to stir the drink before sipping.

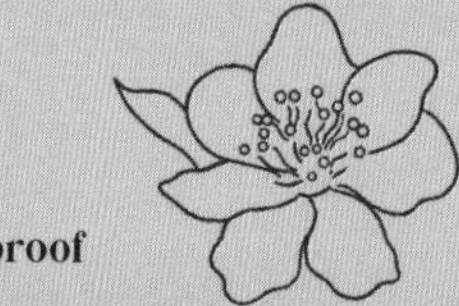

Concerned that psychics, mediums, mind readers and memory stealers threaten the sanctity of your brain? Keep all your thoughts and dreams safe by forgoing alcohol. This mocktail isn't completely alcohol-free because of the Angostura bitters, so leave it out if you want a drink that's 100 per cent zero-proof. Citrus, sharp and tannic, this refreshing mocktail is made with English breakfast tea, but if you'd like a more floral drink, use Earl Grey instead and dash it with bergamot bitters just before serving.

Secret Keeper

Serves 1

60ml (2fl oz) English breakfast tea, cooled

30ml (1fl oz) fresh lemon juice

15ml (½fl oz) Demerara Syrup (see page 11)

1 tsp glycerine (optional)

15ml (½fl oz) egg white or aquafaba

Angostura bitters, to garnish

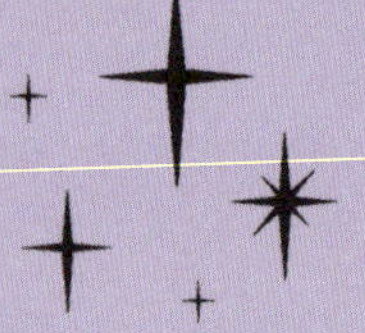

Place a coupe glass in the freezer to chill for 5–10 minutes.

Pour the cooled breakfast tea, lemon juice, Demerara Syrup, glycerine (if using) and egg white/aquafaba into a cocktail shaker. Half fill the shaker with ice. Seal and shake well for 15–30 seconds, or until the tin is frosty.

Strain the cocktail into a clean, empty glass. Dump the ice out of the tin. Pour the mix back into the shaker, seal and shake for another 30 seconds, or until the tin feels light.

Fine strain the cocktail into the chilled glass. Dot the top with a few drops of Angostura bitters and serve.

Changeling Ingredients

The magic ingredient in this mocktail is glycerine. It gives the drink a thicker, more satisfying mouthfeel. Alcohol has a rich texture that's often missing from zero-proof drinks. Adding glycerine gives alcohol-free drinks a similar richness.

A happy ever after is the dream. And yet – after the enemies have become lovers and the battle has been won – if there's a hint of trouble in the supporting characters' faces, that can only mean one thing: another book in the series! Bad news for the main characters, but good times for the readers. This easy-to-mix mocktail also has a subtle hint of danger lingering in it thanks to the Crodino, a syrupy Italian soft drink that's as bitter as Campari but without the booze. It adds a tart aftertaste to the ruby grapefruit juice, creating a sherbetty drink with a sharp sting.

HAPPY FOR NOW

Serves 2

100ml (3½fl oz) Crodino, chilled

200ml (7fl oz) fresh ruby grapefruit juice

Grapefruit wedge, to garnish

Fill two highball glasses with ice. Divide the Crodino between the two glasses. Top each glass up with 100ml (3½fl oz) grapefruit juice and stir.

Tuck a grapefruit wedge into each glass and serve with reusable straws.

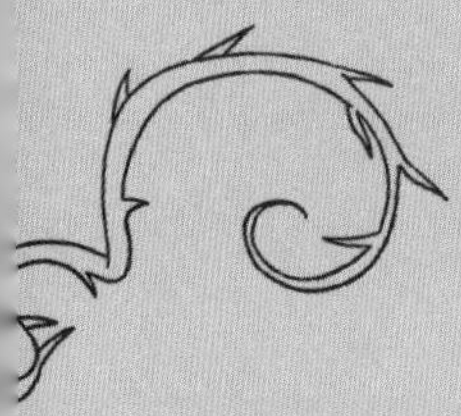

If you can't be better than them, be worse. Dive into the shadows with a pack and make the darkness your own, either by becoming adept at wielding infernal powers or by getting really good at making coffee. Both skills will bring people to their knees. And one is a little bit easier to master than the other. An iced coffee on a hot day is pure brunch bliss. This coffee cocktail combines cold brew with the gentle fizz of ginger beer and a splash of sharp lime. A light, bright coffee blend is going to be the best match for this mocktail. Look for coffees that promise sharp citrus and berry flavours.

Bound By Shadows

Serves 6

300ml (10fl oz) Cold Brew Coffee (see right)

90ml (3fl oz) fresh lime juice

45ml (1½fl oz) Demerara Syrup (see page 11)

300ml (10fl oz) ginger beer, chilled

Lime wheels, to garnish

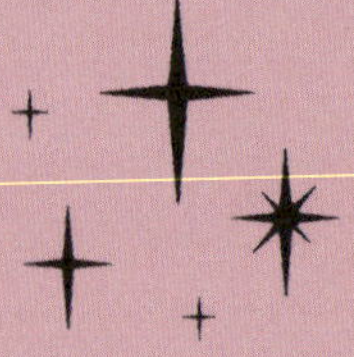

Half fill a large pitcher with ice. Pour in the Cold Brew Coffee, lime juice and Demerara Syrup. Gently stir to mix.

Drop in a handful of lime wheels and stir them through the ice. Top up the pitcher with the ginger beer. Serve in collins glasses with extra ice.

Make Your Own Cold Brew Coffee

Steeping coffee grounds in cold water over a few hours gives you a smooth coffee that's full of the bean's natural flavour. You can vary the ratio of water to coffee and the amount of steeping time to get a weaker or stronger brew. A good starting place is 1 tbsp filter coffee grounds steeped in 300ml (10fl oz) cold water for 12 hours. Strain the coffee and transfer to a clean bottle or jar (for how to sterilise glass jars or bottles, see page 11). Store it in the fridge for up to a week.

Copper-coloured hair and a bad temper? Colour me interested. Whether it's a badass FMC with scarlet braids, a brooding MMC flicking red hair out of his jade-green eyes, or a sassy, strawberry-blonde sidekick, gingers will always have a place in my heart. This alcohol-free cocktail was created in tribute to them. The mix of cranberry and pomegranate juice is bright red, crisp and fruit filled. The hot sauce and the splash of brine from a jar of pickled chillies gives it a hit of spice, but you can add more if you want it hotter.

Spicy Red Head

Serves 1

50ml (1¾fl oz) cranberry juice, chilled

45ml (1½fl oz) pomegranate juice, chilled

A dash of pickled jalapeño brine

75ml (2½fl oz) lemon and lime soft drink, chilled

A few dashes of hot sauce

Lemon wheel and pickled jalapeño coin, to garnish

Fill a collins glass with ice. Pour in the cranberry and pomegranate juice. Add a dash of jalapeño brine. Stir to mix.

Top up the drink with chilled lemon and lime soft drink. Add a few dashes of hot sauce. Briefly stir. Taste and add more hot sauce or jalapeño brine, if you'd like it hotter.

Thread the lemon wheel and pickled jalapeño coin onto a cocktail pick and rest it on the glass. Serve with a reusable straw.

Dragons don't answer to humans, but people have to meet the expectations of their firedrakes all the time. Courage, strength, resilience, purity of heart, intelligence, ancestry, commitment, loyalty – the list of personal qualities that dragons get picky over is long. If the pressure of a dragon's baleful inspection is getting to you, refresh your resolve with a glass of salted yuzu lemonade. Crisp and fruity, this homemade non-alcoholic soda has an extra layer of savoury richness thanks to the pinch of black salt that's stirred in. A drink to share with the riding squad.

Dragon's Judgement

Serves 4

60ml (2fl oz) fresh lime juice

60ml (2fl oz) yuzu juice

4 tbsp caster (superfine) sugar

½ tsp black salt

600ml (20fl oz) soda water, chilled

Lime wedges, to garnish

Pour the lime and yuzu juices into a small pitcher. Add the sugar and black salt (use more or less salt, depending on how sulphurous you'd like your mocktail to be). Stir well for a few minutes until the sugar has dissolved.

Fill four highball glasses with ice, then pour in the salted lime and yuzu juice. Top up with chilled soda water and gently stir to mix.

Tuck a lime wedge into each glass and serve with reusable straws.

Changeling Ingredients

Black salt, or kala namak, is a mineral-rich rock salt with a distinctive, sulphurous flavour. Savoury and sour, it enhances the drink's zingier flavours. If you can't find it in your local shops, swap in a pinch of Himalayan pink salt or use flaky sea salt. You can leave the salt out entirely if you'd prefer a fresh, sweet yuzu lemonade.

PITCHERS

A mate bond that snaps into place the moment you look at someone is romantic, but it's not as much fun as a relationship that slowly builds until the MCs (and the readers) are on their knees with anticipation. Slow-burn romances can be sweet and mild or sizzling with heat – how high you set your spice rating is up to you. The same can be said for this zero-proof mocktail. It's based on a sangrita, the Mexican version of a virgin Mary. You add heat to the drink with a mix of hot sauce, black pepper and Tajín. You choose how fiery you want it to be. If you like things alcoholic, serve a shot of chilled silver tequila on the side.

Slow Burn

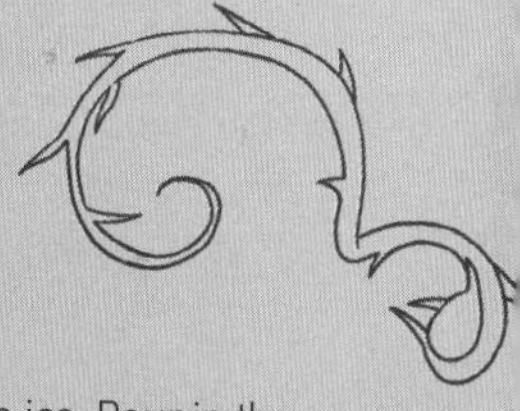

Serves 4

1L (35fl oz) tomato juice, chilled

500ml (18fl oz) fresh orange juice

50ml (1¾fl oz) fresh lime juice

1 tbsp hot sauce

½ tsp freshly ground black pepper

½ tsp celery salt

2 tsp Tajín Clásico seasoning

Lemon wheels and jalapeño coins, to garnish

Half fill a large pitcher with ice. Pour in the tomato juice, orange juice and lime juice. Gently stir to mix.

Add the hot sauce, black pepper, celery salt and Tajín. Stir to mix, then taste and add more hot sauce if you'd like it spicier.

Serve in rocks glasses with extra ice, garnished with lemon wheels and jalapeño coins.

If romantasy has taught us anything, it's that the quiet, bookish people are the ones you should worry about. Behind the mild manners, the librarians, book lovers and scribes all have feral hearts. This harmless-looking iced tea is exactly the kind of cocktail they would go for. Delicious sipped from a dainty cup while cataloguing parchments, it's made with a combination of English breakfast tea and Demerara Syrup, which gives it a biscuitty nuttiness that's lightened by the lemon juice. Two types of liquor and a generous measure of sparkling wine add some oomph.

Scribe's Punch

Serves 4

500ml (18fl oz) English breakfast tea

120ml (4fl oz) London dry gin

120ml (4fl oz) St Germain elderflower liqueur

60ml (2fl oz) fresh lemon juice

15ml (½fl oz) Demerara Syrup (see page 11)

400ml (14fl oz) dry sparkling white wine, chilled

Lemon wheels, to garnish

Brew the tea, then set it aside to cool.

When you want to mix the drink, pour the tea into a large punch bowl or pitcher. Add the gin, St Germain, lemon juice and Demerera Syrup. Add a few cupfuls of ice and stir well to mix.

Top up the punch with the chilled sparkling white wine. Add a handful of lemon wheels and stir through to mix. Serve straight away in punch cups, teacups or thick-stemmed wine glasses.

Family barbecues with eskies of beer, nights out hunting as a pack, and early mornings curled up with their mate – werewolves like to keep their pleasures simple. If you've got your sights set on a shifter, you're not going to impress them with liquor-loaded cocktails or a range of fine wines. Hit the coolers instead and whip up a pitcher of this beer cocktail. It's based on a radler, the German version of a shandy. A refreshing mix of lager and lemonade, splashing in a generous measure of bourbon gives it extra heft. The bourbon's vanilla and oak flavours add a hint of ice cream to the finished drink. Delicious shared on hot days with the pack.

Pack House Punch

Serves 6

150ml (5fl oz) bourbon

900ml (1½ pints) lager, chilled

450ml (15¾fl oz) sparkling lemonade, chilled

Lemon wheels, to garnish

Pour the bourbon into a large pitcher and add two cupfuls of ice. Stir well to chill the bourbon.

Top the pitcher up with the chilled lager, then the chilled lemonade and lemon wheels. Briefly stir to mix.

Serve in ice-filled old-fashioned glasses with a lemon wheel floated in each glass.

Whether you're looking for a dose of courage, a dash more glamour or just want a bit more rhythm on the dance floor, faerie wines always deliver. This vibrant, blossom-rich version is made with a dry sparkling white wine. Look for fizzes that promise notes of pears, citrus and red apple – they'll pair brilliantly with the gin, elderflower liqueur and lemon juice that give this drink it's kick. Add a pinch of golden drink shimmer or flakes of edible glitter for the full faerie effect.

Faerie Fizz

Serves 6

210ml (7fl oz) London dry gin

180ml (6fl oz) St Germain elderflower liqueur

60ml (2fl oz) fresh lemon juice

510ml (18fl oz) dry sparkling white wine, chilled

Gold drink shimmer, to garnish

Pour the gin, St Germain and lemon juice into a large mixing glass. Half fill it with ice. Stir well for 1 minute to mix and chill.

Strain the gin and St Germain mix into six flute glasses. Top each glass up with chilled sparkling white wine.

Add a pinch of gold drink shimmer to each glass and lightly stir to swirl it through the fizz. Serve straight away.

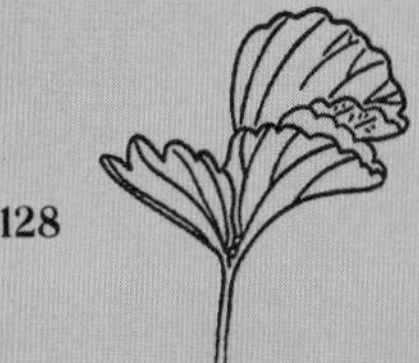

There comes a time for every FMC when she has to choose between the blond or the brunette. Does she want a wickedly good-looking shadow daddy who'll push her to her limits, or the radiantly handsome teddy bear who'd never leave her side? Luckily for you and your friends, all you have to decide between is a pale yellow citrus shot or a smoky spiced tot of rum. Pick your destiny.

You Have to Choose

Each cocktail serves 6

For the Blond Shots:

120ml (4fl oz) lemon vodka

60ml (2fl oz) triple sec

60ml (2fl oz) yuzu juice

60ml (2fl oz) Simple Syrup (page 11)

For the Brunette Shots:

150ml (5fl oz) dark rum

50ml (1¾fl oz) dry vermouth

50ml (1¾fl oz) sweet vermouth, such as Punt e Mes

12 dashes of black walnut bitters

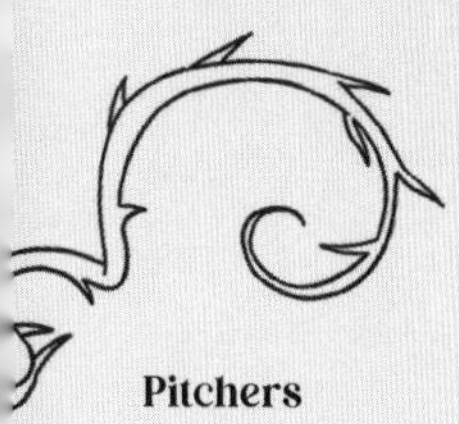

Sterilise two glass bottles, following the method on page 11.

To make the Blond Shots, pour the lemon vodka, triple sec, yuzu juice and Simple Syrup into a sterilised bottle. Seal and shake to mix, then chill in the fridge for at least 6 hours but ideally 24 hours. It will keep for up to a week.

To make the Brunette Shots, pour the rum, dry vermouth and sweet vermouth into a sterilised bottle. Dash in the black walnut bitters. Seal and shake to mix, then chill in the fridge for at least 6 hours but ideally 24 hours. It will keep for up to a week.

To serve, let people choose which path they'd like to go down and pour them a shot.

Changeling Ingredients
Swap the black walnut bitters for chocolate bitters if you'd prefer a sweeter dash of spice in your drink.

The ballroom is lit by starlight, and the lords and ladies glitter with jewels. Take to the dancefloor and twirl with the high fae while the music still plays, then run when shadows curl at the edge of the room. Until trouble comes, what's one more waltz and another glass of that delicious wine punch they're serving? Pale pink and bursting with lush fruit flavours, this lightly sparkling white wine sangria is a heady drink. The lime juice ensures the passion fruit and pineapple don't end up too sweet, while the ginger beer adds a delicate touch of spice.

Summer Ball Sangria

Serves 6

2 lemons

2 limes

120ml (4fl oz) passion fruit liqueur

60ml (2fl oz) fresh lime juice

500ml (18fl oz) sauvignon blanc

250ml (8¾fl oz) pineapple juice, chilled

750ml (26¼fl oz) ginger beer, chilled

Slice the lemons and limes into wheels and scoop them into a large pitcher. Pour in the passion fruit liqueur, lime juice and sauvignon blanc. Gently stir to mix, then set aside for 2–3 hours to steep.

When you're ready to serve, add 2 cups of ice to the pitcher. Pour in the pineapple juice and stir well to mix. Top up the pitcher with the ginger beer. Serve the sangria in ice-filled rocks glasses.

The longest day is always a good excuse for a party in the fae courts. An enchanted evening when everyone can relax and enjoy the extra hours of sunlight, the warm weather and plenty of good food and drinks. If you're planning your own seasonal celebration, make a batch of this easy-drinking fruit punch. Essentially a DIY Pimm's, but with vodka rather than gin in its base mix, it can be easily doubled, tripled, quadrupled or more. And you can also prepare the mix of vodka, triple sec and vermouth ahead and keep it chilling in your fridge, bringing it out when you're ready to start mixing drinks.

Summer Solstice Cup

Serves 6

150ml (5fl oz) vodka

150ml (5fl oz) sweet red vermouth

150ml (5fl oz) triple sec

1 orange

1 lemon

1 apple

½ seedless cucumber

A small bunch of mint

125g raspberries

850ml (29¾fl oz) sparkling lemonade, chilled

Pour the vodka, sweet vermouth and triple sec into a large pitcher.

Slice the orange and lemon into thin wheels. Quarter the apple, slice out the core, then cut it into thin slices. Slice the cucumber into thin rounds. Add the prepared fruit and veg to the pitcher, and gently stir to mix. Set aside for 1–2 hours to steep.

To serve, pick the leaves off a small bunch of mint and add them to the pitcher with the raspberries. Add a few cupfuls of ice. Top up with the chilled lemonade and gently stir to mix.

Serve in rocks glasses with extra ice.

Save time: travel by portal. Hopping from realm to realm through magic gates, mystic pools and enchanted mirrors is a faster way to journey. Beware of culture shocks – not every world is happy to welcome you. Some are even waiting to attack. Approach this aniseed-heavy sparkling cocktail with a similar level of caution. It looks appealing – glittering with gold flakes and sweetened with Chamomile Syrup – but there's a twist of absinthe hidden in its depths, which makes it stronger than your average glass of fizz.

Through the Portal

Serves 6

90ml (3fl oz) absinthe

120ml (4fl oz) Chamomile Syrup (see page 12)

720ml (25¼fl oz) dry sparkling white wine, chilled

Edible gold glitter, to garnish

Pour the absinthe and Chamomile Syrup into a mixing glass. Half fill it with ice. Stir for 45 seconds to 1 minute to chill.

Strain the absinthe mix into six flute glasses. Top up each glass with chilled sparkling white wine.

Add a pinch of edible glitter to each glass and lightly stir to swirl it through the drink. Serve straight away.

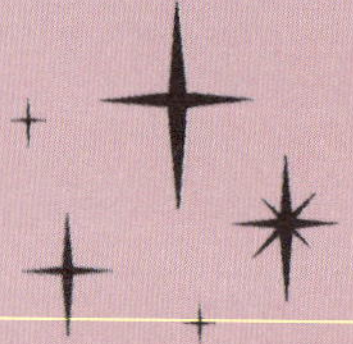

If every court in the fae realms gets a party to celebrate the seasons shifting, then it's only fair we do a little carousing too. This cosy, warm fruit punch is the winter equivalent of the Summer Solstice Cup (see page 135). It's simply spiced with cinnamon, which gives it a comforting, nostalgic flavour. The mix of brandy, triple sec and sweet vermouth helps perk the drink up. Adding the spirits to the apple juice once it's warmed through means you don't lose too much of the alcohol.

It's the Lore

Serves 6

1 apple

1 orange

3 cinnamon sticks

1L (35fl oz) apple juice

150ml (5fl oz) brandy

150ml (5fl oz) triple sec

150ml (5fl oz) sweet vermouth

Slice the apple into wedges and the orange into rounds. Place them in a large pan and add the cinnamon sticks.

Pour in the apple juice. Set the pan on a medium heat and warm until it's steaming but not bubbling.

Turn down the heat to low and cover the pan with a lid. Gently heat for 10 minutes. Take off the heat. Add the brandy, triple sec and sweet vermouth. Ladle into mugs or heatproof glasses, and serve.

This iced coffee cocktail looks normal – safe, even. A milky frappé sweetened with condensed milk and topped with a swirl of whipped cream. But it hides a secret: a punch of oak- and vanilla-rich bourbon that means this coffee milkshake has a secretly boozy heart. It's not the same as having to conceal your world-changing magical abilities from a society that would tear you to pieces if they knew the truth, but it's close. Best to foreworn your friends before they take their first sip.

Hidden Powers

Serves 4

100ml (3½fl oz) bourbon

900ml (30fl oz) Cold Brew Coffee (see page 114)

400ml (14fl oz) sweetened condensed milk

400ml (14fl oz) full-cream (whole) milk

Whipped cream, to garnish

Pour the bourbon, Cold Brew, condensed milk and milk into a high-speed blender. Blitz on high for 30 seconds to 1 minute, until the drink is whipped and frothy looking.

Fill four collins glasses with ice. Pour in the coffee frappé. Top with whipped cream and serve with reusable straws.

There's always time for a side quest. A trip somewhere dangerous to recover a mystical object, or a quick sojourn back to the mortal realm to visit family. Even a night out at a local tavern, carousing with the locals. B plots always move the main story along and, although you might be screaming for the MCs to get on with the important business, we'd miss the distractions. This side-plot take on a French martini serves up a shot of sparkling wine alongside the main drink – a pineapple and raspberry cocktail. Is the drink still good without the fizz? Yes. But it's not as much fun.

SIDE QUEST

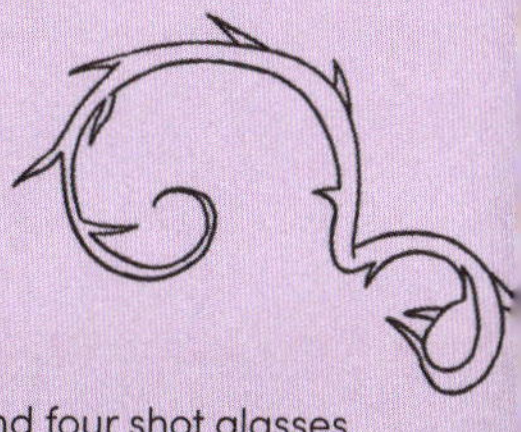

Serves 4

250ml (8¾fl oz) pineapple juice, chilled

100ml (3½fl oz) vodka

100ml (3½fl oz) raspberry liqueur

20ml (¾fl oz) fresh lime juice

100ml (3½fl oz) dry sparkling white wine, chilled

12–20 raspberries, to garnish

Place four martini glasses and four shot glasses in the freezer to chill for 5–10 minutes. Thread raspberries onto four cocktail picks – 3 to 5 raspberries on each pick should be about right.

Pour the pineapple juice, vodka, raspberry liqueur and lime juice into a large mixing glass. Half fill it with ice and stir well for 1–2 minutes to mix and chill.

Strain the cocktail mix into the chilled martini glasses. Rest the cocktail picks with the raspberries on the side of each glass.

Pour 25ml (⅘fl oz) chilled sparkling white wine into each shot glass. Serve together. You can depth charge the shots of sparkling wine in the cocktail (if you're going to do that, serve the cocktail in large coupes rather than martini glasses). Or you can sip it, shoot it or just pour the wine into the martini glasses to top up the cocktail.

Romantasy Cocktails

Published by Cider Mill Press, an imprint of HarperCollins Focus LLC, 501 Nelson Place, Nashville, TN 37214, USA.

13-Digit ISBN: 978-1-40035-519-8
10-Digit ISBN: 1-4003-5519-2

Books published by Cider Mill Press Book Publishers are available at special discounts for bulk purchases in the United States by corporations, institutions, and other organizations. For more information, please contact the publisher.

cidermillpress.com

HarperCollins *Publishers*, Macken House, 39/40 Mayor Street Upper, Dublin 1, D01 C9W8, Ireland (https://www.harpercollins.com)

Typography: Abhaya Libre, Belgin, Fallen Angels, Quincy CF, Sofia Pro

Image Credits: Illustrations by Louisa Maggio

Printed in Malaysia

25 26 27 28 29 PJM 5 4 3 2 1
First Edition

For Rebecca O'Donnell, who showed me the way

Thanks to
Mark Campbell for suggesting
I work on *Romantasy Cocktails* with him
and being a brilliant guide throughout the
process. Rachel Cramp, my wonderful editor,
who is a dream to work with and improved
my copy a thousandfold. Louisa Maggio,
whose gorgeous illustrations have brought this
book to life. Mietta Yans, designer extraordinaire,
for pulling the whole book together. Tessa King for her
sharp proofreading skills, and everyone at HarperCollins
who has worked so hard on this book. Thank you to
my friends and family for their ongoing support
and willingness to be cocktail guinea pigs.
And special thanks to The Dragon & Spice
Smutty Book Club, who helped me fall
hard for romantasy – your advice and
encouragement have been invaluable.